POKéMON™

Galar Region
Gigantamax Clash

POKéMON™
Galar Region
Gigantamax Clash

Adapted by R. Shapiro

Scholastic Inc.

ISBN 978-1-338-74653-2

10 9 8 7 6 5 4 3 2 1   21 22 23 24 25

Printed in the U.S.A.
First printing 2021

CHAPTER 1

Here they are!" Professor Cerise said. He was standing in the Cerise Laboratory in Vermilion City, holding up two colorful tickets. He handed them to Ash and Goh with a smile.

The boys examined the tickets. "The World Coronation Series?" Goh read aloud, very excited. "And not just that, but tickets to the *finals*! That's cool!"

"Isn't it?" Professor Cerise agreed.

Ash didn't understand. He hadn't heard of the World Coronation Series. "What's cool?" he asked.

Goh and Professor Cerise were shocked.

"Wait . . . Ash, you really have no idea?" Goh asked, skeptical.

Ren and Chrysa, who worked at the lab, were sitting nearby and noticed the commotion. Ren jumped in to explain. "Up until now, each region has had its own League, or Championship, each with its own Champion," he told Ash, who knew all about that already.

Chrysa continued, "But at the World Coronation Series, they choose the top Trainer from everyone around the world!"

"That *is* really cool!" Ash said.

Goh waved his ticket under Ash's nose. "And these are for the finals!" he added. "Tickets to the big showdown!"

"Then . . . then . . ." Ash was starting to put it all together. "That means we'll get to see the world's best Pokémon battle for ourselves!"

"Exactly," Professor Cerise confirmed.

"Wow!" Ash cried. What an incredible opportunity!

"Piiika!" Pikachu was excited, too!

"It takes place in the Galar region," Professor Cerise explained. "And there are things that will happen in that stadium that will awe and amaze you! I want you to go and take in everything you possibly can."

Ash and Goh were ready. "Great! Thanks, Professor. I can hardly wait!" Ash said. He loved Pokémon battles!

"And while I'm there, I'll catch *tons* of Pokémon!" Goh said. His goal was to catch one of every kind of Pokémon. He'd been to the Galar region before, but he couldn't wait to meet more new Pokémon on this trip. His partner, Scorbunny, leaped up onto his shoulder happily.

They were off to see the World Coronation Series!

Their flight to the Galar region was mostly uneventful. But once the two friends entered Galar airspace, all the lights on the plane suddenly shut off.

Everyone looked around in confusion. What was going on? The flight attendant asked the passengers to remain calm. Everyone stayed seated, but there was a lot of anxious murmuring.

"Something's out there!" Ash said. "I can feel it!"

Goh wasn't so sure, but he and Ash peered out the window. Soon, they saw a huge line of spikes sticking out of the clouds. Something massive was hidden beneath. Electricity crackled around it.

A moment later, the lights came back on in the plane, and everything was back to normal.

"Whatever we passed by . . . what was it?" Goh asked Ash.

"It was a Pokémon!" Ash replied.

"I thought so," Goh said. "It had real power, for sure!"

"Scorbun!" Scorbunny agreed.

"Really gets the ol' blood pumping, doesn't it?"

Ash said cheerfully. "Just think of all that mystery . . . and it's in the Galar region, waiting for us!"

"Yeah—it got my blood pumping, too!" Goh agreed, giving Scorbunny a big hug.

After the plane landed, the boys and their Pokémon pals took a bus into the city of Wyndon. By the time they arrived, it was evening.

Ash stretched his arms up and announced, "Hey there, Galar region! I'm back!"

Pikachu was excited to be there, too. *"Pika-chu!"*

Goh turned to Scorbunny on his shoulder. The Rabbit Pokémon was originally from Galar. "You haven't seen Wyndon in a while," Goh said.

"Scor!" Scorbunny agreed, happy to be back.

Ash was eager to get to the battle. "Hey, Goh, which way is the stadium?" he asked.

"There! Right in front of your face!" Goh replied.

Ash walked forward, but all he could see was a big wall. "Uh, where?" he asked.

Goh chuckled. "Look up . . ." he said, tilting Ash's head backward.

That's when Ash realized what he was looking at. The big wall was just the bottom of an enormous, rose-shaped stadium! There was a big arch stretching over the entire thing.

Ash gasped. "It's huge!" he cried. He and

Pikachu started running around the stadium toward the entrance, with Goh and Scorbunny close behind. They weaved through the crowd— there were a lot of people still outside, meeting friends or stopping at vendors on their way in.

"Awesome! Awesome! Awesome!" Ash cheered as he ran.

Right before the entrance stairs, Goh stopped and pumped his fist in the air with a laugh. "This is a great place to catch some Pokémon!" he declared.

Ash didn't want to get sidetracked, though. "Hey, Goh, we're hitting the stadium!"

"Well, *I'll* be out catching Pokémon," Goh tried to protest.

But Ash grabbed his arm and dragged him up the stairs and inside. It wasn't every day that they had tickets to such an amazing event!

In the stadium, rows and rows of benches surrounded a huge field with matching Poké Ball crests decorating each side. The stadium was open to the air, and stars twinkled in the night sky above. As Ash and Goh took their seats, they marveled at the size of the crowd.

"So many people . . ." Ash said.

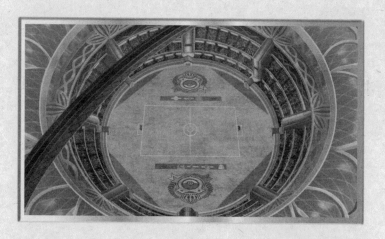

"A lot more than I ever imagined!" Goh agreed.

But they weren't the only ones noticing the crowd. A few rows back, Team Rocket—Ash's longtime enemies—spotted Ash and Goh sitting down.

"Twerps? In the middle of *this* place?" Jessie said. She, James, and their Pokémon Meowth and Wobbuffet were all in regular street clothes as a disguise.

"Normally, I'd be suggesting we steal Pikachu . . ." James said.

"But when the Boss gives a direct order, we put the normal stuff aside," added Meowth.

Jessie clarified their orders. "We're to steal the Galar Pokémon who grow to gigantic size!"

"Yes. For a giant prize!" James said.

"Right!" Meowth said. Holding up their black Rotom Phone, he added, "And this time, we've got the right phone for the right job!"

"Wobbb-buffet!" Wobbuffet agreed. Team Rocket's Patient Pokémon always agreed with them.

Just then, the stadium's lights dimmed, and

everyone looked to the field. The audience cheered as a spectacular light show started in the middle of the battlefield—flashing beams and spinning circles of light in many different colors. The lights kept changing to new shapes, patterns, and hues as the announcer began speaking.

"Welcome, everyone!" his voice boomed. "It's the moment you've all been waiting for! We're here to witness the world's largest, world's greatest Pokémon battle, to determine the world's greatest Trainer! Welcome to the World Coronation Series!"

Sparkling fireworks began going off in the stadium in addition to the colorful beams of light coming from all different directions. The announcer continued, "So, how did we get here? The Masters Eight, the top Trainers ranked by the Pokémon Battle Commission, have entered this competition of high-stakes battling so that they may vie for the much-coveted title of Monarch! But who, you may wonder, are our two finalists?"

The stadium went dark, and a spotlight

appeared over a man walking out onto
the battlefield. He had spiky red hair and a
dark cape.

"First up, I introduce to you . . . Lance!" the
announcer said. The crowd gave a big round of
applause.

Ash was excited to see his friend. "All right,
it's Lance!" he cried.

"Representing the Kanto region!" Goh
cheered.

The announcer continued, "Lance is one
of the Kanto League's Elite Four and winner of
the prestigious Elite Four Cup! Lance emerged
victorious from the Trainer's ultimate dream,

the Pokémon World Tournament in Driftveil City! Lance showed his attack skills as a member of the Pokémon G-Men! His use of Dragon-type Pokémon has been described as battling art! A world-class Trainer with world-class Pokémon!"

Then a spotlight came on over a man striding out on the other side of the battlefield. He had purple hair and a fancy cape.

"I am now pleased to introduce our other finalist. It's . . . Leon!" the announcer said, and the crowd went wild. "Born and raised in Galar and known for winning the Galar Champion Cup

on his very first try in battles that weren't even close! One who has never tasted defeat! A Trainer who takes on any challengers—even once taking on a hundred challengers from throughout the world, and beating every single one of them! The king of the kingdom! The superstar of Galar! The undefeated Champion, Leon!"

The stadium lights came back on in a burst. Lance and Leon were in position across from each other on the battlefield.

"It won't be long now," Goh said. He and Ash were ready for action!

CHAPTER 3

The referee floated down to the center of the field on his Aegislash. "We will now begin the final match of the World Coronation Series!" he said. "Will both Trainers come forth?"

Lance and Leon stepped forward, and the referee explained the rules. "The battle will be a single match. A Trainer wins when the opposing Trainer's Pokémon cannot continue."

Lance addressed Leon. "I've seen your previous battles. I can tell that you're a Trainer with considerable skill. That's why I knew that you'd be the one to eventually join me here."

"Can you feel it, Lance?" Leon said, closing his eyes and swooping his arm down. Lance was confused, but Leon kept talking and gesturing widely. "To witness the tense, still air

on the pitch, the opposite from the audience cheering and yelling . . . both fantastic, wouldn't you say?"

Lance chuckled, and Leon continued, "But remember, the audience is also a bit cruel. They want nothing more than to see one of us lose, after all! But I love pushing past the fear. I love giving it everything I've got as a Trainer!" Leon swooped his cape around dramatically in front of his face. "It's the greatest feeling, and I can't get enough of it!"

Lance looked at him in disbelief. "You think you've already won!"

Leon explained, "The reason I'm unbeatable

is because I learn from every battle I see or take part in. And today—I'll learn. From my victory!" He and Lance stared at each other fiercely.

"There's no need for words now," Lance said, pulling out a Poké Ball. "We will battle to determine who's stronger!"

The referee called, "Please bring out your Pokémon!"

Leon hurled a Poké Ball into the sky. A Charizard burst out and let out a mighty roar.

Lance spun his Poké Ball forward, and a Gyarados appeared, baring its fangs. But

instead of having blue scales, the Gyarados was red.

Goh and Ash were ecstatic. "Incredible! Look at the color of that Gyarados!" Goh shrieked.

The play-by-play announcer set the stage. "It's Leon's undefeated ace Pokémon, Charizard, and, evolved from a gold Magikarp, Lance's red Gyarados!"

"Scor, scor, scorbun, scorrrr!" Goh's Scorbunny was very excited!

The referee gave the signal above the field. "Battle begin!"

"The time has come!" Lance said.

"Indeed," Leon responded. "Let's have a champion time!"

The crowd cheered, and the Trainers commanded their Pokémon.

"Now, Charizard, Flamethrower!" Leon called. Charizard leaned back with a roar, preparing its flame.

"Gyarados, counter it with Hyper Beam!" Lance cried. Gyarados reared back to unleash its move.

The two powerful attacks met head-on in the middle of the field, until, with a burst of

smoke, Gyarados's Hyper Beam overpowered Charizard's Flamethrower.

"Dodge it!" Leon called to his Pokémon. Charizard soared into the sky as Gyarados tried to hit it with Hyper Beam. Charizard successfully dodged the beam and landed back on its side of the battlefield.

"I must say, Gyarados, you are just as strong as I suspected," Leon called. "All right, Charizard, use Air Slash!"

Charizard's wings glowed bright as it charged forward through the air.

"Block it, Gyarados!" Lance called.

Gyarados slammed its tail into the ground, sending huge chunks of the ground into the air. They collided with the Air Slash in a flash of light and dust.

"Look at that!" the announcer cried in admiration. "As if the kickback from its Hyper Beam were nothing, Gyarados moves to block that Air Slash! That's Lance for you—his training is on a different level!"

"Use Flamethrower!" Leon called to Charizard, who zoomed and sent a Flamethrower so powerful, it propelled itself backward.

"Do it!" Ash cheered.

"How do you deal with that?" Goh asked in disbelief.

As if in answer, Lance called to Gyarados, "Dragon Dance!"

Ash and Goh were riveted.

Gyarados spun around in a flash of purple and orange as the announcer narrated. "There it is! Gyarados uses Dragon Dance to boost its speed and attack strength!" But it wasn't enough. "Flamethrower scores a direct hit!"

"We need to get closer," Lance said to Gyarados. "Take it down using Aqua Tail!"

A spinning column of water surrounded Gyarados's tail. It thrashed upward and smashed Charizard.

"That's *some* power!" Ash said.

Goh was in awe of Lance's strategy. "Even if Gyarados is hit with Flamethrower, it won't be that effective," Goh said. "So it took the attack and used Dragon Dance, and that increased its own speed and power!"

The announcer agreed. "Now, *that* was a super-effective attack!"

Charizard was still recovering. But when Leon asked if it was okay, the Pokémon shook off the hit and got ready for another attack.

Lance said to Gyarados, "Let's follow up. Use Ice Fang repeatedly!" Gyarados's fangs instantly turned to ice, and it surged forward.

"Intense!" the announcer described the action. "Gyarados, after enhancing its power and speed, winds around Charizard in a series of attacks!"

"Throw it off, Charizard!" Leon called. "Then use Fire Spin!"

Charizard roared, then sent a burst of flame that encircled Gyarados. The Atrocious Pokémon looked worried.

"Gyarados is surrounded by Fire Spin and can't move!" the announcer said, impressed.

"You're kidding!" Goh exclaimed.

"What's Lance gonna do?" Ash wondered. This battle was amazing!

"Gyarados, cut your way out using Aqua Tail!" Lance called. Water spun around Gyarados's tail, and it successfully put the flames out.

Ash and Goh were impressed by the powerful move.

Lance was satisfied, too. "Yes!" he said. "Now use Ice Fang!"

Gyarados charged once again at Charizard. But Leon didn't seem worried. "This is what I've been waiting for . . ." he said. "All right, Charizard, use Thunder Punch!"

"What?!" Lance cried. That was not what he was expecting!

Ash and Goh were in awe. "That's an Electric-type move!" Ash yelled.

"Charizard had it in reserve this whole time!" Goh added.

Charizard reared back, crackling with electricity. It blasted Gyarados, who fell to the ground.

"Use Thunder Punch repeatedly!" Leon called to Charizard.

"Pika!" In the stands, Pikachu was surprised to see so much Electric-type action!

Ash couldn't take his eyes off the field. "If Lance lets this go on, then he could lose!" he said.

Lance commanded Gyarados, "Counter with Aqua Tail, repeatedly!"

Gyarados charged toward Charizard. Their attacks clashed dramatically over and over as they roared, dust spinning around them in the air.

"That's awesome!" Ash cried.

Finally, the two Pokémon blasted each other back onto their own sides of the battlefield.

"This battle isn't over yet—I forbid it," Leon said. But instead of calling out another move for Charizard, he held out a Poké Ball. Charizard disappeared back inside it in a purple flash.

"Yes, I couldn't agree with you more," Lance said. Then he, too, held out a Poké Ball and called Gyarados back into it in a purple flash.

"Could this be?" the announcer asked. The stadium crowd waited tensely to see what would happen next.

CHAPTER 4

Lance held out his Poké Ball. "All right! Gyarados, ready?" A purple flash sparked from his wristband and zipped into the Poké Ball. With a bright burst, the outside of the Poké Ball became a sparkling web of purple light. It began to get bigger and bigger.

Ash, Goh, and their Pokémon pals were stunned. What was happening?! They'd never seen this before!

"Go, Dynamax!" Lance called, tossing the huge Poké Ball forward. Gyarados appeared under swirling purple storm clouds—then *it* grew bigger and bigger with flashes of purple light. In the end, the Pokémon was truly enormous! It crackled with power and leaned back with a roar.

"There it is! Dynamax Gyarados!" the announcer called.

"Dynamax Gyarados . . ." Ash repeated, in awe.

"I had no idea!" Goh said, amazed. "They use this during battles in Galar?!"

"So when Professor Cerise said there'd be things that would amaze us, he really wasn't kidding!" Ash replied.

Pikachu and Scorbunny hadn't seen anything like it, either. They stared at the enormous Pokémon in wonder.

Team Rocket was impressed, too. "Now, *this* is battling!" Jessie cried.

"Good things come in *big* packages, too!"
Meowth agreed.

James turned to Jessie. "So when the Boss
spoke of giant-sized Pokémon, this is what he
was talking about!"

Jessie was excited—but she'd misheard
what the phenomenon was called. "This Dyna-
socks thing is for me!"

James agreed with Jessie. "Big stockings
isn't what he meant . . ."

"Oy! The word is *Dynamax*!" Meowth
corrected them, rolling his eyes.

Back on the field, Leon spoke. "Dynamax

Gyarados—I like it!" he said. "Now I'll show you what Charizard can *really* do!" He held out his Poké Ball, and just like Lance, his wristband flashed purple. Then the ball sparkled with a web of purple light, and grew bigger and bigger.

Leon tossed the shimmering Poké Ball into the air and cried, "Gigantamax!"

Charizard appeared and then grew, and grew, and grew with flashes of light under swirling clouds. It became just as big as the Dynamax Gyarados! But Charizard had changed aspects of its appearance, too—it had larger claws and wings of flame. It flashed with fire as it let out a huge roar.

"It's Gigantamax Charizard!" the announcer called.

Everyone in the stadium was on their feet. Ash and Goh were astounded, and so were their Pokémon partners.

"That's Gigantamax?!" Goh said, impressed.

"So cool!" Ash cried.

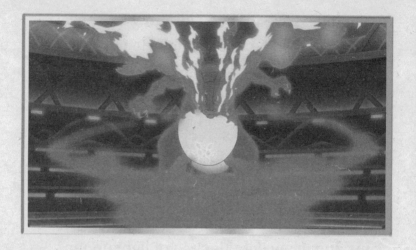

The announcer described the new situation. "This has gone from a normal Pokémon battle to a superpowered Dynamax extravaganza!"

Lance kept the battle moving. "Use Max Geyser!" he called to Gyarados. An intense, glowing stream of water burst from Dynamax Gyarados's mouth.

"The Water-type Max Move, huh?" Leon said as water rained down on the field. "It seems like something you would use. Charizard, meet it using Max Lightning!"

As Charizard glowed and crackled with lightning, a sizzling storm cloud formed over the field. The announcer called, "Max Lightning is the Electric-type Max Move!"

The Max Lightning blasted Gyarados, who fell back in pain.

"Aiming for super-effective hits is the way

to victory!" Leon called. Lance was clearly frustrated.

"Now! Use Max Strike!" Lance commanded Gyarados. It stomped its tail into the ground, sending a jolt toward Charizard.

"Charizard, use Max Airstream!" Leon countered. Before the Max Strike hit it, Charizard flew up and sent a swirling blast of air back to Gyarados.

"It dodged our attack!" Lance said in disbelief. Then Charizard's Max Airstream made a direct hit to Gyarados. The Pokémon roared in pain.

"It's a champion time to turn up the heat!" Leon said confidently. "G-Max Wildfire!"

Charizard flapped its gigantic wings of fire, sending a flame shaped like a bird flying at Gyarados.

"Gyarados, use Max Guard!" Lance called. Gyarados put up a shimmering blue shield. The fire crashed into it, and the entire half of the field was engulfed in a blazing inferno!

When it cleared a moment later, Gyarados was unharmed behind its shield. The announcer said, "Gyarados protected itself from G-Max Wildfire with Max Guard!"

"I wonder . . ." Leon said in response. Then he smiled and said with a bow, "Now, get ready for the last act!"

Gyarados's Max Guard was gone—but the G-Max Wildfire move wasn't over. As Gigantamax Charizard roared, the bird of flame reappeared and swooped around the stadium. It slammed into Dynamax Gyarados once . . . twice . . . three times. Thick gray smoke billowed, and a flash of flame surrounded the huge Pokémon.

To Lance's dismay, Gyarados was overcome.

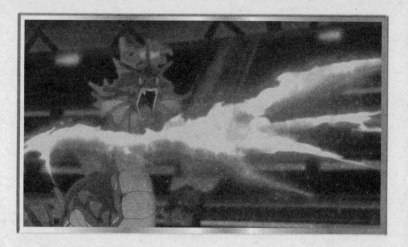

It shrank back down to its regular size and lay on the ground in pain.

The referee swooped over on his Aegislash to examine the Atrocious Pokémon. "Gyarados is unable to battle! So, the winner of this match is Leon!"

The crowd cheered wildly. But Ash was still in shock. "Now, who would've thought that Lance could've lost?" he asked.

On the field, Leon approached his Charizard, who had shrunk back to its normal size again as well. "Charizard, you did very well," Leon said with pride. "Now you and I are true world

Monarchs!" Leon and Charizard high-fived, and then the Flame Pokémon roared in victory, shooting a huge stream of fire up into the sky.

"That was awesome," Ash said. That battle had been far beyond his expectations!

"Pika pika!" Pikachu agreed.

"Yeah! That Monarch Leon is really something else!" Goh said.

"Scor!" Scorbunny added.

On the field, Lance approached his Gyarados. "You were amazing," he said. He held out a Poké Ball, and Gyarados disappeared inside. "Now get plenty of rest."

Lance and Leon met in the middle of the battlefield. Lance seemed unhappy at first, but then he accepted his defeat.

"I guess it's over," he said.

Leon held out his hand so they could shake. Lance had been a great opponent. "That Dynamaxing was amazing," Leon said.

As Lance shook Leon's hand, he explained how he'd learned to Dynamax. "I previously went on a journey to the Galar region and trained at the Dragon Gym. Wearing that historic uniform left a deep and lasting impression, which is why I wear what I wear now."

"I'd say this is a proud moment for them, too," Leon said.

"It's an odd feeling," Lance continued. "I'm not angry I lost. In fact, I'm happy that I witnessed the rise of a great new Monarch!"

"Thank you, Lance," Leon said with a smile. "It was a tremendous battle."

Lance gripped Leon's hand, held it high in the sky, and turned to the crowd as he declared,

"Here today, we've witnessed the rise of the greatest Monarch in the world! If a Trainer has a strong and upstanding nature, their Pokémon will respond! And that's how a Trainer grows strong with their Pokémon—as strong as Leon and Charizard!"

The crowd in the stadium screamed and cheered as the announcer made a final proclamation: "Now, once again, presenting . . . the winner of the World Coronation Series, crowned the strongest in the world! The Monarch, Leon!" Leon struck a victory pose and basked in the applause.

Ash, Goh, and their Pokémon watched, clapping. "So Leon's the strongest Pokémon Trainer in the world?" Goh asked Ash.

"That's right," Ash said. "And I want to have a battle with him!"

"Pika-chu!"

Goh and Scorbunny gasped. It was just like Ash to come up with such a bold goal!

CHAPTER 6

Team Rocket was walking down the stairs out of the stadium. They'd enjoyed the battle, too.

"That's what I call cool!" Jessie said.

"We just saw something amazing!" James agreed.

"But we've gotta get back to stealing Pokémon, stat!" Meowth reminded them.

Wobbuffet was looking the other way. Suddenly, it started waving its arm at them. *"Wobba wobba!"*

A Pokémon they'd never seen before was walking out from behind some nearby bushes. It had a teal body and a brown shell, with a big spike on its forehead.

"Drednaw, drehh," it said in a raspy voice.

Team Rocket all peered at it.

"Who's that Pokémon?!" Jessie asked.

"Let's find out," Meowth said. He got out their Rotom Phone.

"Drednaw, the Bite Pokémon," their Rotom Phone said in a childlike voice. "A Water and Rock type. Um . . . I dunno."

"You don't know?" Jessie said in disbelief. Was that really all the information their Rotom Phone had?

"But it's a Galar region Pokémon," Meowth said.

"So it must grow giant size!" James concluded.

"Perfect for us!" Jessie said.

"All right, come on down!" Jessie and James cried together, reaching joined hands into the air. As they expected, a Pelipper sent by their Boss appeared in the night sky and spit out the familiar robot vending machine full of Poké Balls. It landed right in front of Team Rocket.

"Our secret Rocket Prize Master!" Jessie and James cheered. It would provide them with Pokémon to help complete their mission. All they had to do to activate the machine was use a special coin: the one on Meowth's head! So Jessie and James picked up Meowth and put his charm into the slot.

"Double oy vey . . ." Meowth complained.

Jessie turned the knob, and a purple Poké Ball came out. "Still only one?" she said, disappointed.

James replied, "Yes, but it could mean that when we get only one, it could be huge, like that Wailord!"

"Yay!" Jessie cried, then tossed the Poké Ball. "Batter up!"

A Pokémon appeared with a flash. *"Bellsprout,"* it said. Team Rocket all slumped over in annoyance when they saw what it was—it didn't look very threatening or good at battling to them!

Jessie grabbed the info sheet and read it aloud. "Bellsprout? The Flower Pokémon?!" She crumpled the paper. "All right, show me you've got more than just flower power. Use Power Whip!"

"Bellsprout!" the Pokémon agreed. It narrowed its eyes and leaped into the air. With a flash, one of its leaf arms became much

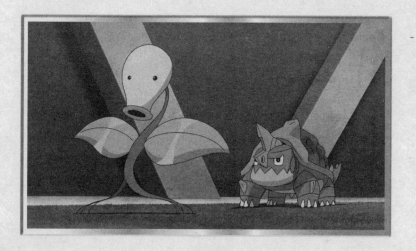

bigger and longer. It whipped the arm down onto Drednaw and knocked it over.

Team Rocket was impressed by the powerful move. "Well, whaddaya know?" Meowth said.

Then Drednaw stood itself back up and gave an angry bellow.

"Now turn that move up to ten!" Jessie commanded Bellsprout.

The Flower Pokémon leaped into the air and struck its glowing leaf arm down again. But Drednaw moved out of the way just in time, and Bellsprout's Power Whip only hit the ground. Then the ground started glowing purple.

"Uh-oh . . ." Meowth said.

A blast of reddish-purple light surrounded Drednaw. Then it started growing, and growing, and growing. Team Rocket started screaming in terror. This was not how they'd anticipated this battle going!

Finally, a Gigantamax Drednaw was in front of them! It glowed red and let out a roar. It clearly was not happy.

Team Rocket was in a total panic—they

started running away as fast as they could. The enormous Pokémon stomped angrily after them. Drednaw's roars were so loud that Ash and Goh heard them from their seats inside the stadium, but they didn't know what the sound was.

When Team Rocket reached the top of the stadium steps, they stopped in front of the entrance and turned around to face Gigantamax Drednaw.

"Jess, sic 'em, quick," Meowth said.

Jessie pulled out a Poké Ball to try to catch the Drednaw. She spun her arm around and

cried, "Poké Ball, don't fail me now!" But when she released it, it just clunked to the ground in front of them.

"This isn't marbles!" James said, annoyed.

Drednaw growled, its enormous face just a few feet away from Team Rocket. They all screamed in terror.

"Bellsprout, attack!" Jessie commanded, pointing at Drednaw. But the Flower Pokémon was nowhere in sight. "Where did you go?" Jessie asked, peering around. She finally spotted Bellsprout behind them, cowering behind a pillar in the stadium's lobby.

"Be-ell . . . sprout . . ." it said, clearly terrified of the Gigantamax Pokémon.

"You sure are quick!" Jessie said, furious that Bellsprout was hiding.

"Drednaaaawww!" Drednaw roared, its eyes glowing red.

Jessie immediately forgot about Bellsprout. She and the rest of Team Rocket were petrified. Their Rotom Phone piped up, saying, "Drednaw.

A not-very-nice Pokémon. Once it starts to chase you, you're toast!"

"We don't wanna be toast!" Team Rocket squealed. They took off running farther into the stadium.

The Gigantamax Drednaw kept chasing them. It was much too big to fit through the doors, so it kept its body outside and extended its neck to ram its head forward. It worked its head farther and farther forward as it roared, shaking the whole stadium.

Ash and Goh looked at each other. They could tell that something major was happening!

CHAPTER 7

Suddenly, Drednaw got stuck in the door-frame.

Team Rocket realized it had stopped moving and turned around to start taunting it, waving their arms in the air. "Nana, nana boo-boo! We're not afraid of you-hoo!"

"Your big head's gotten *too* big!" Jessie said.

Drednaw pulled its head back . . . then pounded it forward again, tunneling even farther into the stadium. By this point, it had gotten through to the battlefield!

Team Rocket yelped and ran away from it, terrified once again. They sprinted across the field, in sight of everyone in the stadium—who were all trying to figure out what was happening.

"What's going on here?!" the stadium announcer asked over the loudspeaker. Leon stood stunned on the field as the announcer tried to explain the situation to the crowd. "A Gigantamax Drednaw, and it's on the rampage!" he said.

Ash and Goh knew they had to try to help.

"Let's go!" Ash said to Goh.

"Right!" Goh agreed.

They grabbed their bags and headed to the exit, each calling to their Pokémon to follow. Pikachu and Scorbunny hurried after them.

Once outside, they ran around the stadium until they were approaching the side of the Gigantamax Drednaw. It had just drawn its neck all the way back into its shell, and it reared up onto its hind feet, towering over them. *"Drednaaawwww!"* it roared.

"Hey there!" Ash called up to it, waving his arms to get its attention. "Ya gotta calm down!"

"If you keep wrecking the place, there won't be a stadium for long!" Goh added.

Drednaw stretched its neck toward them

in an aggressive charge. Both boys and their Pokémon partners screamed and leaped out of the way, tumbling onto the ground.

But Ash stood up right away, determined. "Guess it's time for a Pokémon battle!" he said.

Goh was shocked—was Ash out of his mind?!

Ash explained, "That way, we'll draw its attention and lead it away from the stadium!"

"Pika!" Pikachu was ready to help!

"But how in the world are you going to battle a Gigantamax Pokémon, Ash?" Goh asked, worried.

"Beats me," Ash said.

"You don't know?!"

"I'll give it a try," Ash replied. He was

determined, and Goh's fears weren't going to stop him. "Goh, you stand way back!"

"No way!" Goh replied, crossing his arms. It was Ash's turn to be surprised. Goh explained, "If you're gonna battle, I'll battle too!"

"Scor!" Scorbunny agreed.

Drednaw drew back its head with a growl.

"'Kay, it's a Tag Battle!" Ash said.

"All right!" Goh agreed.

Ash ran forward and planted his feet in battle stance. "Let's do it, Pikachu!"

"We're in on this, too, Scorbunny!" Goh called, running up next to Ash.

"All right! Thunderbolt!" Ash commanded. Pikachu crackled with electricity and sent a jolt right at Gigantamax Drednaw, hitting it in the chin. But the attack didn't seem to affect the huge Pokémon at all. That wasn't a good sign . . .

"Use Double Kick!" Goh commanded Scorbunny. His Pokémon zoomed forward, picking up speed as it ran, until it launched into the air and landed two kicks on Drednaw's face.

Again, they seemed to have no effect.

"Oh, man!" Goh said. Scorbunny was just as frustrated.

Drednaw grunted and drew its head deeper into its shell. Ash could tell it was preparing for a big attack.

"Heads up!" he warned.

"Okay," Goh said, steeling himself.

A moment later . . . *"Drednaawwww!"* the Pokémon roared as its shot its head powerfully forward, right at its opponents.

They stood their ground. "Now use Electroweb!" Ash said to Pikachu. His Pokémon leaped into the air and sent a crackling web of electricity at Drednaw's face. It was a direct hit . . . but Gigantamax Drednaw just shook it off and kept coming at them!

That was the limit. Ash, Goh, Pikachu, and Scorbunny all shrieked and started running away. They were outmatched in this battle!

CHAPTER 8

Ash, Goh, and their Pokémon ran as fast as they could along the path around the stadium as Gigantamax Drednaw extended its neck after them. Just as it was about to reach them . . . it got stuck!

As it spluttered in frustration, Ash and Goh noticed a purplish glow coming up from the ground around them and their Pokémon.

"What's going on?" Ash asked. Pikachu was confused, too.

"I think I know, Ash . . ." Goh said.

To Pikachu's surprise, its tail began crackling with electricity. Suddenly, the purple light was going *through* Pikachu. And just like Gyarados, Charizard, and Drednaw, Pikachu started to grow, and grow, and grow! Soon it was

absolutely enormous! Its tail glowed white, and three red clouds floated around its head.

Ash and Goh were completely shocked. They screamed, and scrambled out of the way of the now-enormous Pokémon.

"Piii . . . kaa . . ." Pikachu boomed. It seemed astonished to be so gigantic!

"Pikachu . . . just Dynamaxed?!" Goh exclaimed. This was wild!

As the huge Pikachu started moving forward, Ash, Goh, and Scorbunny were knocked over by the force of its footsteps.

Ash still couldn't believe what had just happened to his best Pokémon buddy.

He could tell that Pikachu was also disoriented.

Then Gigantamax Drednaw recovered. It reared back on its hind legs, ready to attack. But Ash was still staring at his giant Pikachu with his mouth wide open.

"Over there!" Goh called.

That brought Ash back to his senses. "Pikachu! Use Quick Attack!" he called.

"Pii-kaa-chuuu!" Gigantamax Pikachu confirmed. It glowed purple and stomped toward Drednaw, making the ground shake with each step. But it was so big, it was moving slowly.

Gigantamax Drednaw came crashing down

onto all fours, sending a G-Max Stonesurge
at Pikachu. Ash and Goh gasped as the
ground split open and a wave of water and
wind crashed toward Pikachu, throwing it off
balance.

"Piiiiiiikaaaaa!" Pikachu stumbled . . . but with
a big effort, it regained control, and started
stomping toward Drednaw once again.

Ash and Goh were watching the gigantic
Pokémon nervously. "Hey, Ash, there are still
lots of spectators here!" Goh said suddenly.
This Gigantamax Battle could potentially be
very dangerous with so many people
nearby!

"Yeah . . ." Ash replied. He was focused on the task at hand. "Pikachu, use Iron Tail!"

"Piii-kaaa!" Pikachu grabbed its own glowing tail and started swinging it.

Meanwhile, Leon had come out of the stadium to see what was going on. "Huh, it's a Gigantamax Pikachu!" he said in surprise.

Pikachu smashed its tail down to the ground, sending a wave of steel spikes toward Drednaw. They hit the Pokémon and knocked it over. *"Drednawww!"* it cried in pain.

"Yeah! Way to go!" Ash cheered for Pikachu.

That's when Leon noticed who the

Gigantamax Pikachu belonged to—and that Ash had nothing on his wrist. "It can't be . . ." he said. "That young man! He's in a Dynamax Battle without a Dynamax Band!"

Drednaw reared back and slammed down again. A huge block of rock shot up from the ground in front of Pikachu.

"What's that?" Ash asked.

"It has to be the Rock-type Max Move!" Goh said.

The boys were surprised to hear a voice yelling down advice from up on the stadium balcony. "Ask it to use G-Max Volt Crash!"

They looked around and saw who it was. "Leon?!" Ash exclaimed.

"Your Pikachu can do it!" Leon called. "G-Max Volt Crash!"

"Okay, I'll try it!" Ash yelled back.

Pikachu was facing Drednaw, looking determined. Just then, Drednaw executed Max Rockfall—it shot its head forward and rammed it into the big rock, tipping it over. The rock was going to fall on Pikachu!

Just in time, Ash called out, "Pikachu! G-Max Volt Crash!"

"Piiiiii-kaaaaaa-chuuuuuuuuuu!" Pikachu leaped up and crashed down to the ground to begin the move. It lit up in a blaze of electricity, sending a flash of lightning up into the swirling dark clouds that had formed above. The clouds crackled, and then the lightning shot back down in an enormous blast, right into Drednaw.

The impact knocked Gigantamax Drednaw into the air and back over a group of trees. It

landed on its shell. With a flash of streaming purple light, the Pokémon shrank back down to its regular size. Then it sat up and looked around, confused.

"Did it work?" Ash asked.

"It sure did!" Goh confirmed. "G-Max Volt Crash . . ."

"Piiiikaaaa!" Gigantamax Pikachu boomed, triumphant. Then, to its surprise, purple light streamed around it, too, and it also shrank back down to its regular size.

Ash ran over to his best Pokémon pal. "You were awesome, Pikachu!"

*　　*　　*

Now that the action was over, Team Rocket popped up out of a bush where they had been hiding.

"Perfect!" Jessie said.

"That Dynamax Pokémon awaits!" James added. Now was their chance to go capture Drednaw!

"Let's move out!" Meowth cried.

"Wooobbuffet!" Wobbuffet agreed, and they all ran off toward where the Drednaw had landed.

*　　*　　*

A moment later, Leon approached Ash and Goh as Pikachu was climbing up onto Ash's shoulder.

"'Scuse me!" Leon said to them. "You're not hurt?"

"Nope, everybody's just fine," Ash said. "Thanks for helping me back there! I really appreciate it."

"Well, I should be the one thanking you," Leon replied.

Ash took the opportunity to introduce himself to such an amazing Trainer. "I'm Ash Ketchum, from Pallet Town," he said.

"I'm Goh, from Vermilion City!" Goh said.

"I'm Leon," Leon said.

"Yeah, we know!" Ash replied.

"Because you're the world's greatest Monarch!" Goh added, in awe.

Ash wasn't going to let this moment pass him by. "You know what? I'd like to ask a favor!" he said to Leon.

Goh gasped. "You're not!" How could Ash be so bold?

Ash asked Leon, "Would you please have a battle with me?"

"Pika-chuu!" Pikachu was just as interested.

Leon looked at the eager young Trainer and his Pokémon with surprise.

"Ash, come on!" Goh said. He was embarrassed by his friend.

Just then, a stadium official walked over to the group. "You know you can't Gigantamax your Pokémon here!" he scolded them. "What do you think you're doing?!"

"I didn't mean any harm . . ." Ash tried to explain.

"Yeah, we were just trying to lure that huge thing away . . ." Goh said, defending Ash.

"Lure it away?" the stadium official asked, confused.

Leon stepped in. "These two are the heroes who saved the entire stadium from ruin!" he said. "At least treat them with respect."

The official looked shocked, and apologized at once.

Leon chuckled and winked at Ash. What a relief to not be getting into trouble!

The next day, Goh, Ash, and their Pokémon partners were sitting at a charming Wyndon café. Goh took a sip of his tea, and then picked up a scone.

"Mmm . . . the scones in Galar are the best you can get *anywhere*!" he said. Pikachu and Scorbunny agreed. They were munching away. But Ash was just sitting and looking dazed, not touching the food.

"Ash, what's wrong?" Goh asked. "I've never actually seen you turn down a chance to eat before!"

"Huh?" Ash said. He was so out of it that he didn't even notice when a Pokémon climbed up next to him on the table. It started scarfing down his scones, its cheeks bulging.

But Goh noticed it! "There's a Pokémon I've never seen!" he cried. He held up his Rotom Phone.

"Skwovet. The Cheeky Pokémon. A Normal type," the Rotom Phone announced. "Skwovet keeps berries in its cheeks, but if its stomach is already full, it can temporarily store food in the tufts of fur on its tail."

The Skwovet was still munching. Goh held up a Poké Ball and tossed it toward the Pokémon. "Poké Ball, go!" With a flash, the Pokémon disappeared inside, and the Poké Ball settled on the ground.

"Skwovet has been registered to your Pokédex!" Goh's Rotom Phone announced.

"Another Pokémon! And this time, it's from Galar!" Goh cheered.

Ash didn't respond. He was still slumped forward in his chair, zoned out.

"Ash, what's bothering you?" Goh asked. "If you want to talk about it, I'm here . . ."

Ash finally seemed to hear him. "Oh, yeah!" he said, looking at Goh. "I was just thinking about Leon's awesome battle yesterday, that's all."

"Now, why am I not surprised?" Goh said with a sigh.

"What's wrong with that?" Ash asked.

Sometimes, Goh found Ash's one-track mind very annoying! But he knew why Ash was so distracted. "This is about how you want to battle Leon, right?"

"Bingo," Ash said, nodding.

"I get it, I get it," Goh said. Then he warned Ash, "You know, trying to get a battle with Leon is not as easy as you think." Ash looked up in surprise as Goh scrolled through his Rotom Phone, confirming information. "Just to get into the World Coronation Series in the first place, you enter online, and then you build up your ranking by having lots of Pokémon battles," he said.

"My ranking?" Ash asked.

"Your position compared to others," Goh explained. "And based on battling records and statistics, the eight highest-ranked Trainers then form what's called the Master Class. At the end of the class match season, there's a tournament where Trainers in the Master Class battle each other, and the winner becomes Monarch!"

"So does that mean that if I submit my entry, then I can battle against Leon?" Ash asked, excited. That didn't sound so hard!

Goh shook his head and said, "It doesn't work that way. Based on whether an entrant wins or loses Pokémon battles, along with the *content* of those battles, entrants get separated into four distinct classes." Goh scrolled on his phone, explaining the breakdown of the three lower classes in the series. Every Trainer started out by being put into the Normal Class. Then they'd battle other Normal Class Trainers to try to increase their rank. Out of all the Trainers who had entered, those who ranked between 999 and 100 became the Great Class, and those who ranked between 99 and 9 were the Ultra Class.

Ash asked which class Leon was in.

"Of course he's in the Master Class!" Goh said. "Not only that, but he's number one! So, Ash, for you to battle him, you'll have to start climbing the ranks to get up to the Master Class."

Ash crossed his arms and thought hard. Pikachu studied him, worried. *"Pika . . ."*

"Sorry if that was a bit too much . . ." Goh said.

But then Ash jumped up from his chair and said confidently, "Well, all I've gotta do is win battles, right?"

Goh laughed. The Ash he knew was back!

Suddenly, Ash realized he was starving. He began stuffing his face with scones—eating so quickly that he started to choke!

Someone handed him a glass of water, saying, "Drink this." Ash gulped it down and soon recovered. But before he could thank the man who had given him the water, he realized who it was . . .

"L-L-Leon?!" he shrieked.

Goh was just as surprised. "Wh-what are *you* doing here?!"

"You said you wanted to battle me, right?" Leon said to Ash.

Ash nodded frantically, and Goh cut in. "But I just finished explaining to him that it wasn't going to be so easy!"

"Being the world's greatest Monarch, I

thought it would be nice to help a young man realize his dream," Leon said with a smile.

Goh just about keeled over in shock, but Ash was ecstatic. "That'd be so awesome!"

*   *   *

Meanwhile, Team Rocket was walking by the Wyndon stadium, totally wiped out. They'd been searching for Drednaw all night, but they still hadn't caught it!

"Talk about a wild waste of a Dynamax chase . . ." Jessie said.

"Leaving us empty-handed and exhausted," James added.

"Where does a jumbo catch of the day find a hiding place?" Meowth finished.

"Wooobuffet," Wobbuffet commiserated.

Suddenly, James noticed a cute little Pokémon hanging off the end of Jessie's hair. It had a tiny shell and a point on the top of its head. "Hey, Jessie! What *is* that thing?" he asked.

"Huh? What thing?" Jessie asked, looking back.

"Who's that Pokémon?" Meowth asked, holding up Team Rocket's Rotom Phone.

"Chewtle. The Snapping Pokémon. A Water

type. When Chewtle evolves, it becomes Drednaw," the Rotom Phone said. Then it added, "Yeah, right. I don't believe it."

Meowth was skeptical, too. "You've gotta be kidding me!" he said. "When this thing evolves, it becomes that huge lug we got a load of yesterday?"

Jessie was happy to hear that. "Hooray! Now grab hold of it, James!" she said, crouching down so he could reach it.

"Uh, or perhaps not," he said, reaching toward the Chewtle very uncertainly. "After all, it's a bit too good at rampaging!" As he

was about to grab it, it chomped on his finger! He screamed in pain and fear, but then he realized . . . "Wait. That doesn't hurt."

Meowth pointed to Chewtle. "Just what we need!" he said. "It's the perfect travel size to bring back to the Boss!"

Jessie and James were thrilled with the idea, and Team Rocket blasted off.

"Say, this is the kind of blast we could get used to!" they cried.

*   *   *

Back inside the stadium, Ash and Pikachu faced Leon in the center of the huge battlefield. The stands were completely empty, but the same referee from the World Coronation Series final was there on his Aegislash.

"Since it's a request from Leon, I'd be honored to referee the match," he said.

"Thanks a lot!" Ash replied.

Leon tossed something small over to Ash. "Ash, take this," he said.

Surprised, Ash caught it and studied it. It was a white band that had a red stripe on the top, a blue stripe on the bottom, and a symbol in the middle. He and Pikachu had never seen one like it before.

"It's called a Dynamax Band. I noticed while you were battling yesterday that you weren't wearing one on your wrist," Leon explained. He pointed to his right wrist, where he wore the same band. "The Dynamax Band gives you complete control over Dynamaxing. Once your Pokémon is Dynamaxed, its move names change, too."

"I'll take it from here," Goh cut in eagerly. He'd read all about Dynamaxing! "The Normal-type Max Move is called Max Strike. The Steel-type Max Move is Steelspike. And the Electric-type Max Move is Max Lightning."

Ash repeated the names of the moves back to Goh to confirm them.

"That being said, your Pikachu is able to Gigantamax," Leon said. Ash and Pikachu

turned to him in surprise. "That means it can use an Electric-type move called G-Max Volt Crash."

"We used that move!" Ash remembered.

Leon smiled. "When you prepare to Dynamax, you send your Pokémon back into its Poké Ball. Then you throw the Poké Ball while channeling the power in your Dynamax Band," he said.

"Pikachu doesn't really like to go into his Poké Ball . . ." Ash explained. He and Pikachu smiled at each other. "We'll come up with something, right?"

"Pika pika!" Pikachu agreed.

Ash slipped the Dynamax Band onto his wrist. "Thank you for the loan. Really!" he said to Leon, who nodded. As Ash admired the band, he chuckled. "This thing is so cool!"

Soon, Ash and Leon were in their places at either end of the field, ready to battle. Goh and Scorbunny stood to the side, tensely watching.

The referee announced, "Now, contestants . . . your Pokémon?"

Ash cried, "I choose you. Let's go, Pikachu!" At the same time, Leon tossed a Poké Ball and called, "All right, Charizard . . . come out!"

Pikachu leaped down from Ash's shoulder, and Charizard appeared in a flash in the air.

"Awesome! Both Pikachu and I really wanted to battle your Charizard!" Ash cheered.

"Pika piiika!" Pikachu agreed.

"It's obvious you understand your Pokémon partner, which makes me happy," Leon said with a smile.

Goh called out some advice to Ash. "In a matchup of types, Pikachu has the advantage!"

"Perhaps," Leon countered, "but when it

comes to Charizard and Monarch Leon, we never lose a battle!"

Charizard roared in agreement.

"That's how we want it!" Ash replied.

The referee called out the start. "Ready? Battle begin!"

CHAPTER 10

Ash was ready to go. "Pikachu! Quick Attack!" he commanded. Pikachu charged forward.

"Charizard! Counter it with Thunder Punch!" Leon called, and Charizard flew ahead with a roar.

The two Pokémon met in the middle of the field, their attacks colliding in a blast of electricity. After a struggle, Pikachu went tumbling into the air, but landed on its feet back on its side of the field, ready for the next move.

"Charizard's power is amazing!" Goh commented.

Ash was frustrated, but eager to try again. "Pikachu, use Iron Tail!" Pikachu's tail glowed white as it spun in the air.

"One more time, use Thunder Punch!" Leon said to Charizard.

Once again, the Pokémon clashed in the air, and once again, Pikachu went flying. Ash was dismayed to see his Pokémon overpowered. But Pikachu landed on its feet, and the battle continued.

"Follow it up!" Leon called to Charizard, who roared and built up another Thunder Punch.

"Electroweb, go!" Ash called to Pikachu. Its sent a glowing web right for Charizard.

"Punch right through it!" Leon said to his Pokémon—and Charizard's Thunder Punch did just that. Ash was disappointed. Right away, Leon commanded, "Now use Air Slash!"

Charizard's Air Slash hit its target with a burst of dark smoke. Pikachu let out a pained cry.

"Pikachu, no!" Ash exclaimed. But his Pokémon again landed on its feet, determined to keep going. "All right! Use Thunderbolt!" he called.

As Pikachu powered up the move, Leon told Charizard to use Flamethrower. Its blast of fire hit Pikachu's stream of electricity and kept blasting. It pushed Pikachu all the way back to its starting spot—though Pikachu hadn't given up yet.

Goh and Scorbunny were worried. How much longer could Pikachu resist Charizard's Flamethrower?

"Do it!" Ash encouraged Pikachu. The Pokémon crackled with electricity, pushing back against the blast of flame. Then Ash's Dynamax Band flashed purple . . . and a stream of purple light started to surround Pikachu! It

grew, and grew, and grew. Gigantamax Pikachu was back!

Its Thunderbolt was much stronger. Finally, it was able to overpower Charizard, who thumped to the ground.

"Charizard?" Leon called. His Pokémon shook off its fall.

Ash was so excited that Pikachu had Gigantamaxed again. "We did it without a Poké Ball!" he cheered.

"Piiii-kachuuu!" Pikachu thundered, stomping its enormous foot.

Leon was happy to see Gigantamax Pikachu,

too. "Amazing. I'm glad we're here!" he said. Then he held out a Poké Ball. "Now, Charizard, return!" Charizard disappeared. Then Leon's Dynamax Band flashed with purple light. The Poké Ball started to glow purple and grow bigger. "This is what I call a real champion time! Gigantamax!" Leon called, tossing the ball into the air.

Charizard burst out, then grew, and grew, and grew. Gigantamax Charizard let out a roar.

"All right, Pikachu, it's time. Use Max Strike!" Ash cried. Pikachu jumped and slammed the ground, sending Max Strike across the field and making Charizard jump back.

"Now Max Airstream!" Leon called to Charizard. It blew an intense swirl of air at Pikachu, who struggled to stay standing.

"Don't let it get to you!" Ash encouraged his Pokémon. Pikachu pushed and pushed against the tunnel of air, but ultimately got knocked onto its back. "Quick, Pikachu, Max Steelspike!" Ash yelled.

As Pikachu slowly sat up, Leon called to his Pokémon. "Charizard, use Max Lightning!" Charizard let out a roar and was surrounded by flame. Pikachu approached, swinging its glowing tail, but it was hit with Charizard's Max

Lightning before it could attack, and it stumbled backward.

"It's time . . ." Ash said. Things were getting serious. "G-Max Volt Crash!"

Pikachu jumped up and pounded the ground, starting the move by sending a bolt of lightning into the churning clouds above.

"Now let's enjoy the finale! G-Max Wildfire!" Leon cried to Charizard. His Pokémon reared back and roared, shooting a bird made of fire directly at Pikachu.

The move hit Pikachu and flames swirled around it as a huge lightning bolt came down and hit Charizard. They were each surrounded by the other's attack.

Goh watched, breathless. "It's a draw," he said. The Pokémon seemed to be evenly matched!

"It's not over yet!" Leon exclaimed.

Charizard eventually shook off the lightning, but Pikachu was tired and couldn't get out from the flames. Charizard blasted another bolt of fire at Pikachu, and another.

"Piiikaaa," Pikachu moaned. Then streams of purple light appeared around it, and it shrank back down to its regular size. It was knocked out.

"Pikachu!" Ash cried, running over.

The referee declared, "Pikachu is unable to battle! Which means the winner is Leon!"

Leon nodded, acknowledging his win. "It's a shame it's over, Charizard," he said to his Pokémon. Then he held out his Poké Ball, and Gigantamax Charizard disappeared in a purple flash.

Ash picked up his Pokémon gently. "Pikachu, you were awesome out there," he said.

Pikachu blinked slowly and then smiled up at its Trainer and friend.

Leon strode over and handed Ash an Oran Berry. "Here, Ash, give this to Pikachu."

Ash did so, surprised at Leon's kindness. "Thank you very much," he said. He also wanted to express his thanks for the great battle. "Leon, I'm really happy that you went all out on me!"

"Battles are no fun when you're *not* going all out," Leon responded with a smile.

Ash took off the Dynamax Band to give it back to Leon. "Thanks for letting me use this," he said.

"You hang on to it," Leon told him.

"Wait, are you sure?" Ash asked, surprised.

"Of course. You're a Trainer who still has rough edges. I like that type," Leon said, and Ash grinned. "But to beat me, you've got a bit of work to do. I want you to break out!"

"Break out?" Ash was uncertain what that meant.

Goh explained as he walked over from the sideline, "It means he really wants you to let 'er rip!"

Leon smiled. "See you," he said with a wave, and started walking away.

"Hey, Leon!" Ash called after him. "Let me have a battle with you in the future, 'kay?"

Leon looked over his shoulder. "The next time, we'll be in a tournament, Ash!"

"Okay!" Ash cried. He couldn't wait.

*   *   *

A few minutes later, Ash and Goh walked out of the stadium together.

"I've decided, Goh!" Ash declared. "See, I'm going to enter this competition and battle Leon again! And I'm gonna win it, too! That'll be my next step to become a Pokémon Master!"

"Perfect!" Goh replied, happy to support his friend. "That plan has 'Ash' written all over it!"

Ash turned to Pikachu on his shoulder. "Buddy? Whaddaya say we get stronger together?"

"Pika pika!"

Ash and Goh looked back at the stadium. Ash imagined his vision for the future: the stands packed with a wildly cheering crowd, all there to watch while he and Pikachu battled Leon and Charizard! Maybe someday . . .

For now, though, Ash was looking forward to his next battle!

POKéMON™

Aliola Region
Battle for the Z-Ring

Pokémon™

Alola Region
Battle for the Z-Ring

Adapted by Jeanette Lane

Scholastic Inc.

CHAPTER 1

For ten-year-old Ash Ketchum, every day was a step on his grand journey to becoming a Pokémon Master. Since he'd arrived in the Alola region, Ash had enrolled in the Pokémon School, where he and Pikachu had met many new friends and Pokémon. Each and every day, they were learning new things and having exciting adventures.

Ash and Pikachu loved exploring Alola. One of Ash's favorite parts of being in a new place was discovering all the new Pokémon. Since they'd first come to Alola, they'd met many new Pokémon friends, and they'd also found a new battling partner for their team. The adorable Rowlet was a Grass- and Flying-type Pokémon with a knack for sneaking up on opponents . . .

and then sleeping away the rest of the day in Ash's backpack.

One morning, Ash was on his way to school when he encountered a Pokémon he hadn't seen before. It stared at him with its intense yellow eyes. Ash gazed right back.

In no time, Rotom Dex gave Ash the lowdown on the Pokémon. "Litten. The Fire Cat Pokémon," Rotom Dex announced, hovering in the air just

behind Ash. "A Fire-type. Litten show few emotions and prefer being alone."

Rotom Dex was a unique companion for Ash. Rotom was a Pokémon that had the ability to live inside various electronic devices. This Rotom was a present from Ash's teacher, Professor Kukui. Rotom had slipped straight from an electrical outlet and into a Pokédex. Now it was an amazing talking device that kept Ash informed about all the unknown Pokémon in Alola. Ash took Rotom Dex with him almost everywhere.

Litten stood on top of a stone wall and kept its steely eyes on Ash. Ash knelt down, trying to lure it his way.

"Litten takes time to build any level of trust," Rotom Dex told Ash.

Ash heard Rotom, but he still wanted to try to make friends with the cute Litten.

Litten jumped down from the wall and approached Ash.

"Hi. What's up?" Ash said, holding out his hand.

Without hesitating, Litten began to rub up against Ash's knees. Pikachu watched from its perch on Ash's shoulder.

"Hey, maybe you're hungry!" Ash said. He opened his backpack and pulled something out. "See? It's my lunch," he explained to the curious Litten.

Ash was excited about the lunch that Professor Kukui had prepared for him. The professor was not only Ash's teacher, but he was also his host. Ash was staying with the professor in his cozy island bungalow for the school year. Professor Kukui was an expert on Pokémon, and he could also make a delicious sandwich.

"Yay! Yummy," Ash said. He tore off a corner of the sandwich and offered it to Litten. "Here you go. It's great!"

"Mrow? Mrow?" Litten looked at the corner of the sandwich in Ash's one hand, and then it looked at the larger part of the sandwich in Ash's other hand. All at once, it leaped for the

larger chunk of sandwich, swiping it right out of Ash's hand. Then Litten tried to escape, but not before Ash grabbed its thick tail.

Litten lashed out with its claws, slapping Ash across the face. Rotom Dex chased it down, but Litten swatted Rotom away with a brisk swish of its tail. Ash, Pikachu, and Rotom Dex watched as Litten trotted off along the stone wall, jumped down, and escaped out of sight.

It was a rough way to start the morning. Plus, now Ash was running late for school!

The Pokémon School was on the island of Melemele, which was one of many beautiful tropical islands in the region. Ash had originally visited Melemele on vacation with his mom. With its strong sun, lush forests, long stretches of beach, and fresh, delicious food, the entire Alola region was a paradise.

Of course, Ash didn't feel like Melemele was paradise that morning. He was really annoyed

about his encounter with Litten. It wasn't just that he'd lost his lunch. Ash sensed something else in Litten, and he wasn't sure what it was. He hoped his friends at school might be able to fill him in.

CHAPTER 2

Wow, so you finally met that Litten," Mallow said. She was standing by the balcony in their classroom. As she looked out over the ocean, the breeze blew through her long green ponytails.

"Is it your friend?" Ash questioned.

"Litten comes up asking for food all the time," Mallow explained. "It's so cute!"

"I fall for it every time!" Lana added. Both Bounsweet and Popplio, Mallow's and Lana's Pokémon, cooed in agreement.

Ash liked Mallow and Lana. He trusted their opinions, but he didn't feel the same way about Litten.

"Well, I don't think it's so cute," Ash said. "That's how I lost most of my sandwich!"

"You mean Litten stole it?" Lillie asked.

"You got it," Ash replied.

Ash's classmates laughed and groaned. They weren't making fun of Ash. They felt bad for him, but the story was pretty funny.

"That sounds like our Litten, all right," Lana said.

"Litten's not the kind who enjoys dealing with people," added Sophocles, another classmate. "It takes a long time to warm up to Trainers, too. They say it's not your average Pokémon."

"That's precisely what I told Ash earlier," Rotom Dex declared.

"You could say Litten's the lone star of Pokémon, right?" said Mallow. "It always seems to be hanging around our restaurant."

"I see it in the market, too," Kiawe said. "It steals all kinds of berries."

"Still, Litten is so cute. I just can't get angry at it." Mallow shrugged.

Kiawe, who was the oldest of the students in the class, seemed less enchanted by Litten than the others. He also seemed to understand Ash's frustration. "So, do you have a plan?" he asked Ash. "To deal with Litten?"

"Someone should teach it!" Ash insisted. "You don't mess with a guy's sandwich!"

"Wait. Teach it?" Lillie asked. "What are you talking about?"

Lillie was the one student who didn't have her own Pokémon. She enjoyed researching Pokémon more than training them.

"Uh, I know just what to do," Ash said with certainty. "I'll catch it!"

All of Ash's classmates were surprised. After everything they had told him about Litten, Ash still seemed to think he could get the stubborn, independent Pokémon to join his team.

The next day, Professor Kukui and Ash were shopping at the local outdoor market. They had already bought lots of fresh fruit and

vegetables for dinner. The teacher was listing the things they still needed to find when, like a flash, Litten ran by.

Just as quick, Ash and Pikachu were on its tail.

"A Litten sighting!" cried Rotom Dex. It began explaining the situation to Professor Kukui.

Litten was quick . . . and sneaky. After racing past several fruit stands, Ash and Pikachu had lost track of the little Litten. Where could it have gone?

"Want to buy some berries, dear?" a kind woman asked Ash. She had gray hair and glasses with thin wire frames.

Ash quickly turned her down. "No, we were looking for a Litten." He scanned the area. "There it is!" he exclaimed, locating Litten just inside the woman's fruit stand. To no one's surprise, it was eating.

As soon as Litten saw Ash, it raised its head and growled. Ash clenched his teeth.

"Now you two," the shopkeeper said, "let's play nice."

"You give it food?" Ash questioned.

"In Alola, nature's bounty is for sharing," the woman said. She bent over and handed Litten a big, juicy berry. "Now, dear, don't eat too fast. I love to feed you, Litten."

Litten looked very content. It trotted off with the berry in its mouth.

By this time, Professor Kukui had caught up to the others. "Does that Litten come here a lot?" he asked the woman.

"All the time," she responded. "A habit, every day. Honestly, I think Litten enjoys looking out for me. That's why I have berries waiting when it comes by for a visit. Now, let me guess," she said, turning to Ash, "Litten made off with some of your food, didn't it?"

"It sure did!" Ash replied. "My sandwich, specially made!" He felt frustrated all over again. If Litten had eaten his sandwich, why was it still so hungry? Why did it need a bowl of fruit and a big berry, too? And why did so many

people like to care for it when it wasn't very nice to them?

"Ash," Professor Kukui said, "I can make you another one." Like Ash's classmates, his teacher wasn't certain why Ash was so upset.

The shopkeeper laughed to herself. "I have no idea where Litten lives, but it certainly is a dear."

CHAPTER 3

The next afternoon, Ash, Pikachu, and Rotom Dex said good-bye to their friends at school and headed for home. They took their usual winding path on a road that looked out over the sea. Melemele Island was so peaceful!

At least, it was usually peaceful. Ash heard some kind of commotion on the hill below. When Ash peeked over the fence on the side of the road, he saw Litten! It was facing off with a much larger Pokémon.

"Rotom, who's that Pokémon?" Ash called out.

"It's a Persian," Rotom Dex responded.

"Persian? It's not like any Persian I've ever seen," Ash replied. Ash had learned that some of the local Pokémon had evolved to look very different from the versions that Ash knew from

Kanto. Ash was familiar with a tan-colored Persian with a red jewel on its head. The Alolan version was gray, and the gem on its forehead was turquoise. They really did look different.

"The Alolan Persian is a Dark-type, so it can be cunning with a bit of a mean streak," Rotom warned.

"But that means that . . . it's gonna . . ." Ash's voice trailed off as he watched the action below with concern.

Persian was advancing toward Litten. Litten was backing away, but it was nearing a steep cliff. Below the cliff, there was only ocean. Litten held a yellow berry in its mouth.

"*Rrrrrraa. Rrrrrraa.*" Persian took a step forward, menacing Litten. Then, all at once, Persian used Fury Swipes, knocking Litten clear off its feet.

"Don't do it!" Ash yelled as he skidded down the rocky hillside. Pikachu was right at his side. "This has gotta stop! Knock it off!" he scolded Persian. "For a single berry, you're being way too rough."

"*Pika!*" Pikachu agreed.

Disgusted, Persian aimed a Power Gem move at them.

Litten tried to pick up its berry and slip away, but Persian wasn't done with the Fire Cat Pokémon.

"*Rrrrrraa. Rrrrrraa!*" Persian had Litten trapped at the edge of the cliff!

"I said knock it off!" Ash yelled out. "Pikachu, Electro Ball!"

Pikachu wound up and pitched an Electro Ball. Persian dodged it. But it was not as lucky when Ash ordered a Thunderbolt. Pikachu's blast landed with a *ZAP*! Persian finally got the message and skulked away.

Ash, Pikachu, and Rotom turned their attention to Litten, who was limping away.

"Hey, Litten," Ash said. "Are you okay?"

"Litten has taken a lot of damage," Rotom Dex said.

It worried Ash to see Litten in pain. "Don't push yourself so hard!" Ash advised. "C'mon, please!"

Pikachu begged Litten, too, but the Pokémon was too stubborn to listen.

Ash walked toward Litten. He knew that the Pokémon was injured, and he wanted to help. At least he could carry the berry for the hurt Pokémon.

But when Ash reached out for the yellow fruit, Litten nipped at him. "Litten? Let's work together," Ash suggested. "We're going to the Pokémon Center."

Litten didn't like that idea one bit. It wrestled away from Ash's hands.

Pikachu tried to convince Litten, but it wasn't until the exhausted Pokémon nearly passed out that Ash could grab hold of it.

Ash promised Litten that he wasn't trying to take the berry away. It was just that Litten needed help so it could recover from its battle.

With Litten still struggling, Ash carried it off. "Rotom, grab Litten's berry!" he instructed. And to Litten, he demanded, "Stop! Quit biting me!"

At the Pokémon Center, Nurse Joy did her
best to bandage Litten so the injuries would
heal properly. She wrapped a bandage
around its back and belly several times. Still,
she was worried that Litten would try to lick
its wounds, so she put a Heliolisk Collar
around its neck. The collar looked like a big disk
that shielded its head. Litten was not happy
about it.

Once she was finished with Litten, Nurse Joy told Ash that it was his turn. "Litten's not the only one who got hurt," she pointed out. Ash looked down and realized he had scratches up and down his arms.

As they prepared to clean up Ash's cuts, Litten sneakily snatched the berry and leaped from its bed.

"Hey, stop!" yelled Ash. He raced after Litten.

"Ash, try to make sure Litten doesn't overdo it!" Nurse Joy called out.

On the way out the door, Ash passed Kiawe.

Kiawe shook his head as he stared after his classmate. "All that for a sandwich," Kiawe murmured.

But for Ash, this was way beyond a sandwich now.

CHAPTER 4

Ash had almost caught up with Litten when the feisty Pokémon tried to jump through an iron fence. But Litten couldn't fit through the bars because of its bulky collar. The dazed Pokémon fell backward on the sidewalk.

Ash stared down at it. "Will you listen to me, please?" he begged. "From now on, no running away! You're not doing what you're told, and it's only hurting you."

Ash scooped up the little Pokémon. He had no choice: he had to take Litten to Professor Kukui's place.

The professor was understanding, as long as it was just for the night. Litten seemed willing to take it easy there. Ash even removed the collar so Litten could relax, and the independent

Pokémon curled up and fell fast asleep in
Ash's lap.

Ash sighed. He wished Litten would trust
him more.

Many hours later, Ash blinked his bleary eyes
open. It was still the middle of the night, and he'd
been sound asleep. He heard a scratching. He
got up and noticed Litten standing by the door.
"Yeah, yeah. I'll open it in a second."

It wasn't until Litten had already bolted out

the open door that Ash really woke up and realized what had happened. Yikes!

"Where's Litten going?" he yelled, rousing Rotom Dex.

"Data is incomplete!" Rotom Dex replied. "Litten's full recovery requires lots of sleep and the absence of stress and strain!"

In no time, Ash, Pikachu, and Rotom Dex were chasing Litten again. They ran down city streets until they came to a remote lane that led to an old, deserted, ivy-covered cottage. Litten ran inside.

Ash, Pikachu, and Rotom all crept inside after it. They saw Litten run to the back room. There, Litten dropped the yellow berry on a table.

"A Stoutland," Ash mumbled, seeing the large Pokémon resting on a couch.

"One that's getting on in years, I'd say," added Rotom.

"I wonder if Litten's been stealing food to bring to Stoutland," Ash thought out loud. That was why Litten needed so much food!

When Litten realized they were there, it turned to face them and hissed. It was clearly protecting the older Stoutland. Ash guessed that the Stoutland had once protected Litten when it was tiny.

As Stoutland munched on the berry, Pikachu reassured Litten that they were there to help.

Ash knelt down next to the two Pokémon. "Guess your dinner's a little late. Sorry, Stoutland," he said softly. "See, Litten got hurt in a fight, so we all went to my place to rest."

Ash took a deep breath and turned to Litten. "Litten, I was hoping I could catch you so you'd be on my team. But now that I see what you're doing, it was a bad plan."

Ash really admired Litten's devotion to its friend. He was glad that he could finally understand why Litten acted the way it did.

Ash looked at Pikachu and Rotom. "We'd better head home. Professor Kukui might get worried," he said. "And next time I visit, I'll bring some food for you." This time, he was talking to Litten. "I can come visit, can't I?"

Just then, they all heard a sound come from outside.

"It appears something is approaching!" Rotom warned them.

"What *is* it?" Ash asked.

The Alolan Persian leaped down from a high window and aimed its turquoise gem at them.

"Quick! Let's get outside!" Ash declared. He, Pikachu, Rotom Dex, and Litten all dashed out the door as Persian sent a blast their way.

Persian pounced and landed right in front of Litten and Pikachu. "Such persistence! There's no doubt Persian is out for revenge," Rotom observed.

Pikachu and Litten bounded forward, ready to defend their friends. "Take it easy," Ash advised them. "Why don't you give it up?" he asked Persian.

Persian growled in response.

Ash called for a Thunderbolt attack. Pikachu aimed, and Litten got ready for its Ember move. But Persian was too quick and attacked Ash with Fury Swipes!

Litten looked concerned, but Ash brushed it off. "A few scratches aren't going to hurt me!"

Persian came at Pikachu and Litten again. Stoutland began to murmur instructions to Litten. It was giving the younger Pokémon battle advice! Litten listened closely.

Litten focused its energy. The bandages wrapped around its belly burst off, and Litten's whole body seemed to pulse with fiery power.

Litten faced Persian and blasted a huge cough of fire for its mightiest Ember ever!

The fireball struck Persian head-on, and the Classy Cat Pokémon raced off, its tail still smoking.

Stoutland gave a gruff huff of approval, and Ash cheered. "That was awesome, Litten!"

Litten gave Ash a little smile. Then it trotted

over to Stoutland, and the older Pokémon looked proud.

"I detect a happy ending," Rotom Dex announced. "Except for you not catching Litten . . ."

But Ash still felt it was a happy ending. He and Litten had an understanding.

The next day, Ash was in for a surprise. He, Pikachu, and Rotom Dex stopped by the ivy-covered cottage to drop off food for Litten and Stoutland. They had two full bags to share, but Litten and Stoutland weren't there.

Where could they have gone? Ash assumed that he must have done something wrong.

Worried, Ash decided to visit the shopkeeper who was friends with Litten. "I feel like it's my fault," he told her.

The woman studied Ash through her wire-framed glasses. "Pokémon are Pokémon, and people are people," she said. "One being's world

isn't exactly the same as the other's. So don't go blaming yourself. Litten's living under the same Alolan sky as you."

Ash thought about her advice. He supposed he needed to try to see things from Litten's point of view. He wondered if their paths would cross again.

Just then, a stealthy black Pokémon with familiar red markings appeared at the shopkeeper's fruit stand. "Litten!" the woman said. "I heard you moved."

Litten looked surprised to see Ash and Pikachu there. Had the three become friends, or was Litten still set on standing alone?

Only time would tell, but it was clear that Ash had learned an important lesson about allowing Pokémon to be Pokémon. It was yet another step on his long journey.

CHAPTER 5

Huh?" Rotom Dex was absolutely confused. It was a school morning, and Rotom was ready to pester Ash until he finally got out of bed, but Ash was already awake. "What have you done with the Ash who sleeps late?" the device asked.

"I can't wait until I can use a Z-Move again!" Ash announced from his bed. "Which means I'm gonna have to get myself a Z-Crystal." He got up and threw on his clothes.

After Ash's experience with Litten, he had decided to focus on his original goal for his time in the Alola region. He wanted to earn another Z-Crystal so he and Pikachu could master their very own Z-Move.

Ever since he had seen Kiawe and Charizard

do their Z-Move, Ash had been fascinated by the special skill. To do a Z-Move, a Pokémon Trainer needed to possess a Z-Ring, which was a kind of bracelet that Trainers usually earned only through a set of complicated tasks called the Island Challenge.

To Ash's surprise—and that of all his classmates at the Pokémon School as well—Ash had received a Z-Ring from the Island Guardian named Tapu Koko. No one knew why the mysterious Legendary Pokémon had given him a Z-Ring. The Z-Ring already had a powerful Z-Crystal inside.

It was an awesome, unexpected gift, but the Z-Crystal had exploded after Ash's first attempt to do the special Z-Move. Oddly enough, the crystal had shattered during Ash's first battle with Tapu Koko.

Now Ash needed to earn another one. He and Pikachu were ready to do whatever it took to take this next step on their journey together.

At breakfast, Ash shared his plan with Professor Kukui.

"A Z-Crystal?" his teacher asked.

"Yeah," Ash confirmed. "I want to get a whole lot stronger and then have a rematch with Tapu Koko." In his mind, he pictured Tapu Koko. The Island Guardian was yellow, with a big orange crest on its head, wide wings, and bold markings that made it look like a warrior. "I can't wait to try those Z-Moves again. Right, buddy?"

"*Pika, pika!*" Pikachu was in full agreement.

"You're as fired up as if you were hit by a Blast Burn!" commented Professor Kukui.

Ash nodded as he took a bite of breakfast. "I remember Kiawe saying that you can earn Z-Crystals by going through the Island Challenge."

"Well, that isn't the only way, but it is the most certain way," Ash's teacher said. He seemed pretty excited about the topic, too. "The key to success is passing the grand trial of each of the islands' kahunas."

Ash gulped down some milk. "So how do you do that?" he asked.

Rotom Dex nudged his way in front of Professor Kukui. "I will answer that with pleasure! A grand trial is a battle between the Trainer and the island kahuna. If the Trainer wins, the kahuna acknowledges the Trainer's worthiness."

"Whoa," Ash said. "Sounds like fun!"

"Fun?" the professor questioned, pushing Rotom aside. "You're up against a kahuna, so if you're overconfident, you can get yourself hurt! And—"

"According to my data," Rotom interrupted, "a grand trial is preceded by lesser trials that must be overcome first."

"Got it. First some little trials, then *BOOM*!" cried Ash.

"All right, all right," Professor Kukui said, seeing Ash's enthusiasm. "I think we should go pay a visit to Hala. He is the kahuna of Melemele Island."

"Right!" Ash cheered.

"*Pika! Pika!*" Pikachu exclaimed.

Soon Professor Kukui, Ash, Pikachu, and Rotom were on their way. Little did they know that there was trouble brewing close by. A pack of Rattata and Raticate had devoured a whole crop of Pinap Berries.

When the farmer and his dog came out to chase the pesky Pokémon away, the pack scampered out of the field and started to stampede across a nearby street. Then the Rattata and Raticate ran right in front of three

Tauros who were pulling a heavy load on a trailer. The Tauros had to stop so fast, their cargo of lumber toppled over and blocked the entire road.

When Ash and the others came across the scene, they had no idea what had happened. "What's going on?" Ash wondered.

"I'd say it was an accident," Rotom Dex replied.

"Attention!" Officer Jenny called out. "This road will be closed until the timber can be

removed. Until that happens, please use a different route."

Ash frowned. He wondered what could have caused the accident. It was frustrating. He didn't want any delays in his new plan to earn a Z-Crystal. Why did there have to be an accident on this road, on today of all days?

Professor Kukui approached Officer Jenny and asked if she could tell them what had happened. The officer recognized him at once.

"Professor Kukui!" she said. She then explained that the whole problem was the fault of the menacing Rattata and Raticate. Ash was amazed that Pokémon could be responsible for such a mess.

"Are you a student at the Pokémon School?" Officer Jenny asked.

"Yeah, my name's Ash," he replied.

"*Pika! Pika!*" Pikachu put in.

"This is my partner, Pikachu, and Rotom Dex," Ash continued.

"I'm Officer Jenny. Glad to be at your

service." She raised her hand to her head in a salute. "Actually, I'm a graduate of the Pokémon School, too."

Ash's face lit up. "Wow! That's so cool!" he exclaimed. Then the excitement of the crowd distracted him. Everyone was in awe of a massive Pokémon's strength as it helped move the timber off the road and back onto the trailer. It was Hariyama. Ash hurried toward it. "You're so strong! Those logs are like twigs to you!"

Ash was amazed to see a man lift one of the logs. He had a broad white mustache and white hair that was pulled in a ponytail on the back of his head. The man wore a yellow robe with wide sleeves and a white belt tied in a large knot at his waist.

"This gentleman is Hala," Professor Kukui told Ash. "He is the island kahuna."

"Thanks a lot, Kahuna Hala," Officer Jenny said.

"Of course," the man responded. "It's my job to solve any problems the island may encounter."

Ash stared in amazement. This man was the island kahuna? And he was there to help with the accident that had stopped Ash and Professor Kukui? Could it really be a coincidence?

"I have a cleanup crew on their way here now," Officer Jenny assured the kahuna, pointing to a pickup truck. "And there they are."

A group of four Machamp jumped from the back of the truck. They immediately formed an assembly line. Each Machamp used all four arms to pass two logs at a time. It took only a

few minutes for them to load all the logs back on the trailer.

"Thank you for all your cooperation," Officer Jenny called out to the crowd.

Ash took the chance to talk directly to the kahuna. He wanted to let him know of his plans. "I'm actually here for the Island Challenge," Ash explained.

"I'm well aware of that," Kahuna Hala replied. "I've been waiting," the older man continued,

"so why don't you and the professor come by sometime soon?"

"We certainly will, sir!" Professor Kukui assured him.

The very next day, Ash and Professor Kukui showed up at Kahuna Hala's home.

"Oh, that was fast," Hala said when he answered the door. "Please come in." He gave Professor Kukui, Ash, Pikachu, and Rotom Dex a tour of his home. When they passed his office, Ash noticed a shelf where several Z-Rings were displayed.

Hala noted that Ash had eyed the powerful rings. "Yes," he confirmed. "The Z-Ring you are now wearing is one that I made."

Ash was shocked. He had not realized that Kahuna Hala crafted Z-Rings. "You made it?" he questioned. "But I got it from Tapu Koko."

Hala nodded solemnly. "I thought that might be the case. One day, I noticed that one of

my Z-Rings could not be accounted for," he explained. "Then I realized it was the work of Tapu Koko."

"Has something like that ever happened before?" Ash's teacher asked, curious.

"This is the first time Tapu Koko's ever taken a Z-Ring, that's for sure," Hala answered with certainty. "It appears Tapu Koko has a strong interest in you, young man."

"Huh?" Ash was confused by Kahuna Hala's comment.

"I'm just talking to myself," the kahuna responded. By this time, they had all settled down on the comfortable couches in the kahuna's living room. The kahuna's Hariyama joined them.

Ash decided it was time to get down to business. "Kahuna, I'd like to get a Z-Crystal as soon as I can. I'll need it for when I battle Tapu Koko again."

"Again?" Hala repeated. He paused for a moment. "Ash, if you don't mind, I'd like you to answer a question for me."

"A question? For me?" Ash wondered what the older man meant.

"I assume you now know that the people of this island have been troubled by a rash of wild Rattata and Raticate. Am I right?"

"Yes, sir," Ash answered.

"If you were the person being asked to solve this problem," Hala continued, "what would you do?"

Ash couldn't answer right away. Professor Kukui chuckled to himself, as if he knew that the kahuna would expect Ash to tackle this kind of challenge.

"I know!" Ash declared. "I'd take Pikachu and Rowlet and challenge them all to a battle, then—"

"My young Ash," Hala interrupted. "Are you interested in learning why the Island Challenge was started so many years ago? You see, it wasn't simply to make Trainers stronger in battle. It was to raise young people in such a way that they will love and protect the islands of

Alola as well as the many people and Pokémon who inhabit them."

What Kahuna Hala said made Ash thoughtful. "Love all that's here and protect it," Ash murmured. Pikachu curled up on Ash's lap.

Hala looked seriously at Ash. "I want you to look for answers that won't *only* lead to battle. We'll talk about the Z-Crystal after I've heard what you come up with."

Ash closed his eyes and put his arms behind

his head. He tried to figure out the Rattata and Raticate problem.

"During my trial," Professor Kukui shared, "I spent quite a long time thinking about Hala's question, too."

"During your trial?" Ash asked.

"Yeah," Professor Kukui confirmed.

Kahuna Hala laughed at that. He knew Ash must be surprised that he had also been in charge of the Island Challenge for Ash's teacher. "Food for thought, huh?" He smiled. "Instead of rushing through things and answering right away, why not take your time and think it over?"

Ash sighed and thought about Hala's question some more.

The next day at Pokémon School, Ash was still thinking. In fact, he was thinking so much that his classmates were amazed.

"Ash has been thinking about something for that long?" Mallow said. Her Pokémon partner, Bounsweet, was sitting on her shoulder.

"Incredible," Lana commented.

Ash had his head down on his desk, and he was moaning in pain—the pain of thinking especially hard.

Finally, Kiawe couldn't take it anymore. "All right, please tell us what Kahuna Hala said."

Ash's head was still down, and his eyes were closed. He looked depressed.

Kiawe sighed. "We may even be able to help you out."

Ash's eyes popped open.

"All you have to do is let us know what he said," Lillie assured him.

Ash told them everything he knew about the Rattata and Raticate, and he explained that his solution could not include a traditional Pokémon battle.

Lillie, who loved to research, suggested they

learn more about Rattata and Raticate. "That information might give us a clue," she offered.

"I believe that's my cue," Rotom said, swooshing in. Ash grabbed hold of the device so he could see the screen better. His classmates gathered around his desk.

Ash was surprised to see the differences in the Alolan form of the long-toothed Pokémon. Somehow, the Alolan forms of these Mouse Pokémon seemed more menacing and fierce.

"Rattata and its evolved form, Raticate," Rotom Dex began. "The Mouse Pokémon. A Dark- and Normal-type. When they band together, Rattata and Raticate steal food from people's homes. Long ago, they came here to the Alolan islands aboard cargo ships, and eventually grew into the Pokémon we see today. The numbers of Rattata and Raticate grew so large that Yungoos and Gumshoos were brought in from a different region to chase them off."

"That's it!" the group of friends cheered.

CHAPTER 7

I see," Kahuna Hala said to Ash when he visited the very next day. "You're saying if we ask Yungoos and Gumshoos to help us, we can all solve the problem together?"

"Yes, sir!" Ash responded.

"Now, that's a thoughtful and wise answer. It's my answer, too."

"All right!" Ash exclaimed. He wondered what would happen next.

"Now, I must be honest and tell you my question was to test whether you had what it takes to go through the actual trial itself," Hala explained.

Ash was surprised to hear that. "Then I should be honest and let you know that I found

the answer together with all of my friends," he confessed. "I hope that wasn't wrong."

"No, not at all," Kahuna Hala responded. "When we are searching for life's answers, we should always look to our friends for help. That in itself is a very important life lesson!"

Ash breathed a sigh of relief.

"Then, shall we go?" Hala asked. He stood up and led Ash out the door.

They soon arrived at the mouth of a great

cave. Kahuna Hala paused in front of the cave and informed Ash of the plan, which had several stages. "There are many Yungoos and Gumshoos living in this cave," he explained. "They are all very strong, but there is one Gumshoos who is so amazingly powerful. It is called the Totem Pokémon."

"Totem Pokémon?" Ash repeated.

"Yes. There are several Pokémon in Alola who have that name. Most of them are following the lead of the Island Guardians, as they assist Trainers who undertake the Island Challenge." Hala peered at Ash to see if the young Trainer was following his explanation. "So, Ash, your trial is to take on the Totem Pokémon in a Pokémon battle and be victorious. Then, if you succeed, I want you to chase away the Rattata and Raticate with the aid of the Totem Pokémon."

As soon as he finished, Kahuna Hala stepped into the moss-lined tunnel that led to the cave.

"But wait," Ash said, running to catch up. "Why would Gumshoos team up with me?"

"Never fear!" Hala said, striding ahead. "If you can earn the Totem Pokémon's respect during your battle challenge, it will assist you in your time of need." They stepped into a giant cavern. "I will be watching. I will be the referee during your trial."

Ash looked around at the great space. Lush plants grew down the walls of red rock. There were several tunnels that led deeper into the hillside. Misty sunlight streamed in through two openings in the cave ceiling.

"It's huge," Ash said under his breath. For the first time, he wondered if he was prepared for this challenge.

"Totem Pokémon Gumshoos." Kahuna Hala's deep voice echoed through the cave. "You have a trial goer! Do your duty and grant him his trial!"

"I'm Ash Ketchum from Pallet Town!" Ash's voice sounded small after Hala's announcement. "I'm asking you for a battle!"

"I can hear something," Rotom Dex said. Ash and Pikachu looked around, wary.

Two Pokémon appeared from the large tunnels on the higher level.

"Are they Totem Pokémon?" Ash asked. While they had sharp teeth and appeared to be fast and strong, they were not especially large.

"No, Ash, they are not," Hala said. "They're the Totem Pokémon's allies. You'll still have to battle them, however. We shall now begin the Pokémon battles that make up this trial!"

Ash sighed. While he would have to battle the two Pokémon before him, it would only be the first round. The Totem Pokémon would come later. "Is there any data?" Ash asked Rotom.

"But of course!" Rotom answered. "Yungoos, the Loitering Pokémon. And Gumshoos, the Stakeout Pokémon. Both are Normal-types. Yungoos have sturdy fangs and jaws, and when they evolve into Gumshoos, they gain a certain tenacity and patience."

Ash listened closely. "In that case, Pikachu, I choose you!" he shouted.

Pikachu strode into position.

"You, too, Rowlet!"

Rowlet bounced out of its Poké Ball and onto . . . the ground.

"It's asleep!" Rotom observed.

Sure enough, Rowlet was snoring. Ash charged forward. "Wake up!" he cried. Rowlet's eyes popped open. The other two Pokémon were already threatening.

"All right, Pikachu, Thunderbolt, let's go!" Ash instructed. "Rowlet, use Tackle!"

The battle was fast and furious. Both sides were fighting well. Gumshoos used a Sand Attack on Pikachu. Yungoos went after Rowlet, who tried to dive away from a dirt blast.

With bursts of power shooting back and forth, the battle continued. Yungoos and Gumshoos created clouds of dust with their moves, making it hard for Ash's team to see. When they came at Pikachu and Rowlet with a double

Hyper Fang Attack, Ash directed his partners to dodge it.

"You're not the only ones who can hide in your moves," Ash called out as Rowlet let off a whirlwind of glowing-green Leafage that spun around its opponents. "Pikachu, Iron Tail!" Ash commanded.

Then Rowlet soundlessly sneaked behind Gumshoos and Yungoos. "Yes!" Ash cried. "Rowlet, Tackle, let's go!"

Pikachu and Rowlet wore down the other two with move after move. At last, Hala announced it was over. "Yungoos and Gumshoos are unable to battle!"

The battle had been so intense, it was hard to believe that it was just the first round of Ash's trial.

A rumble filled the cavern. The sound of massive footsteps vibrated off the ground and stone walls. The footsteps were followed by a mighty roar.

Ash, Pikachu, and Rowlet stood close together, nervously waiting for their next opponent.

There!" Hala declared. "This Gumshoos is truly a Totem Pokémon."

Ash gazed on his next opponent with amazement. "It's so big!" he exclaimed.

"Unreal!" was Rotom Dex's opinion. "This one is three times the size of the previous Gumshoos!"

Ash, Pikachu, and Rowlet were not only overwhelmed by Totem Gumshoos's size, but they were soon overwhelmed by its power, too. Pikachu used Thunderbolt, but Totem Gumshoos whacked it with Frustration.

"That Gumshoos's speed is immeasurable!" Rotom Dex reported.

Rowlet raced in and used Tackle to distract Gumshoos while Pikachu recovered, but

Gumshoos picked up a rock and thwacked Rowlet, too.

Ash raced to Rowlet's side. "Thanks a lot, Rowlet! You got Pikachu out of a jam!" he said, rubbing his partner's soft head. The brave Pokémon was stunned. "Take a rest! Return." Ash said, and Rowlet disappeared inside its Poké Ball.

At once, Ash had to get his head back in the battle. He took a stance and called to Pikachu. "Pikachu, Electro Ball!"

"*Pika, pika, pika!*" Pikachu focused its power and shot a mighty, pulsing Electro Ball at Totem Gumshoos, but Gumshoos simply knocked the ball out of the way and returned a Sand Attack move.

"Pikachu, no!" Ash yelled, seeing his partner tumble and skid across the cave floor.

Pikachu grunted, but got right back up.

Ash was determined, too. "Pikachu, use Quick Attack!"

Rotom was surprised by Ash's call. "I don't think using Quick Attack will have any effect at

all," the device yelled, but Pikachu was already in action.

Pikachu bounded ahead. When Totem Gumshoos sprang a Sand Attack, Ash instructed, "Pikachu, use that Sand Attack! Now!"

Pikachu raced through the sand, using it as cover, whizzing all around and confusing Totem Gumshoos.

"Now!" Ash yelled again, and Pikachu started landing Quick Attack moves again and again and again.

Once Totem Gumshoos was exhausted, Ash directed Pikachu to use Thunderbolt. Pikachu began to glow with intense energy, and it zoomed toward Totem Gumshoos.

"*Pika-chuuuuuuuuuu!*" the little Pokémon cried.

Totem Gumshoos grunted, and then toppled onto the ground with a crash.

"The trial is over! I declare that the challenger, Ash Ketchum, wins!" Kahuna Hala announced.

Ash celebrated with Pikachu and Rotom Dex, but his attention was soon drawn to Totem Gumshoos. It was still on the ground.

"Totem Gumshoos!" Ash approached the giant Pokémon.

Rotom Dex lingered behind, worried that it was unsafe, but Ash went right up to Gumshoos and leaned over it. "Totem Gumshoos, are you all right?"

Trying to get up, Totem Gumshoos pushed Ash out of the way. But with its other hand, it offered something to Ash.

"*Gumshoos, gumshoos, gum,*" the Totem Pokémon said solemnly.

Ash reached out. It was a Z-Crystal!

"For me?" he asked. "Really?"

"*Gumshoos, shoos shoos gum.*" The Totem Pokémon insisted Ash should take it.

"Wow," Ash said. "Thanks a lot."

He stared at the magical gem in his hand.
It was white with a single black swirl. That
marking meant it was for the Normal-type
Z-Move. "It's a Z-Crystal, and it's all mine!" he
cheered.

Watching the exchange, Kahuna Hala was
impressed. It was very rare for a Totem
Pokémon to give a challenger a Z-Crystal, and

he believed Ash must be a most unusual Trainer.

Even though Ash was thrilled to have earned a Z-Crystal, he hadn't forgotten what Hala had told him was the final stage of his challenge.

"Excuse me," Ash said, looking up at Totem Gumshoos. "I was wondering if you'd help us chase off all of the Rattata and Raticate."

Totem Gumshoos nodded in agreement.

Getting rid of the pesky, long-toothed, greedy Pokémon was far easier than the earlier stages of Kahuna Hala's trial. The next day, a group met Officer Jenny at an old warehouse where the Rattata and Raticate had been feasting. With the help of Totem Gumshoos and his allies, Ash and his team were able to chase all the unwanted Pokémon away.

Professor Kukui and Officer Jenny couldn't believe how easily Ash's new Pokémon friends defeated the nasty Mouse Pokémon.

"As kahuna of the island of Melemele, I'm very happy to verify that you have indeed passed the trial," Hala told Ash. "Your next step is the island's grand trial. Ash, I'm really looking forward to it, and to see your Z-Move in battle with my very own eyes."

"I'm really looking forward to it, too!" Ash admitted.

Pikachu looked just as thrilled. Of course, the grand trial meant battling Kahuna Hala himself! Ash knew it would be a tremendous challenge, but he was ready for it.

Ash's good work with Totem Gumshoos and its allies ended up in the Melemele newspaper, and he earned a certificate of appreciation from Officer Jenny. It was very exciting, but for Ash, it was all part of his journey to become a Pokémon Master.

His next big step was the grand trial, and Ash didn't want to waste any time. He planned to battle Kahuna Hala the very next day.

The grand trial included a certain amount of ceremony. Part of the ceremony was for both opponents to meditate together at a temple called the Ruins of Conflict, which was deep in

the forest. Pikachu and Hala's partner, Hariyama, were there, too.

"Today we will perform a grand trial battle with our young challenger, Ash. I now ask Tapu Koko, guardian of conflict, to bestow upon us the power of Alola . . . of all the islands."

"Please, Tapu Koko," Ash added. "This will be my grand trial with Kahuna Hala, so I want you to watch it!"

The two future opponents closed their eyes and remained silent.

Ash had a hard time staying still. His arms felt stiff, and his foot itched! But he tried to concentrate—for Tapu Koko. Ever since the Island Guardian had given him his first Z-Crystal, Ash had felt a bond with the mystical Pokémon. True, he wanted to one day be able to battle the powerful Pokémon again, but he also wanted to be worthy. He wanted to believe that Tapu Koko recognized something special in him.

After a while, Kahuna Hala chuckled to himself. "You can move now, Ash," he said.

"Do you think Tapu Koko heard us?" Ash asked the kahuna.

"I would say there's a good possibility Tapu Koko heard us," he replied. "But as Island Guardians go, Tapu Koko follows its own path."

At that moment, there was a shrill coo that echoed through the leafy forest. Ash was certain that their ceremony had had a special guest!

After their meditation, Ash and Hala met back up with Professor Kukui and Rotom Dex at the outdoor battle arena. It was a simple stone battle space, without stands or fanfare, surrounded by palm trees.

"All right, Ash," Professor Kukui coached him. "One thing before your grand trial begins. Do you know the correct poses to use the Normal-type Z-Move?"

The professor's question referred to the

specific Z-Crystal that Ash had received from Totem Gumshoos. It allowed him to do just one of several kinds of Z-Moves.

"I sure do!" Ash assured his teacher. "We practiced till it's second nature. Right, Pikachu?"

"*Pika, pika!*" Pikachu agreed.

"Yes, he is correct," responded Rotom Dex.

"Way to lock on and master your Z-Move!" the professor said.

"I can't wait to use it!" Ash replied.

"When you use your Z-Move," Professor

Kukui advised, "both you and your Pokémon expend a large amount of energy. So with the way you, Pikachu, and Rowlet are now, your Z-Move should be quite tiring."

Ash listened closely. "The important thing is *when* I use it, is that right?" he confirmed.

"Exactly, Ash," Professor Kukui said. "We're ready, Hala!"

"It's truly an honor to battle you!" Ash and Kahuna Hala said at once. Then the grand trial began!

"Ready to go, Rowlet?" Ash asked. "I choose you!"

Rotom Dex was certain Rowlet would be asleep when it appeared from the Poké Ball. But Rowlet was wide awake and ready to battle.

"Crabrawler, come out!" Hala said, summoning his first Pokémon. Crabrawler was a low-to-the-ground Pokémon with four legs and two mighty pincers.

"Crabrawler?" Ash questioned. "Rotom?"

"My greatest pleasure," Rotom replied, pulling up the data. "Crabrawler, the Boxing Pokémon. A Fighting-type. Crabrawler is always aiming to be number one. It will guard its weak spots with its claws in battle and throw punches while looking for an opening. Since Rowlet is a Flying-type, it's a good match for our side!"

"Great!" Ash replied, preparing himself.

At once, Hala called his first shot. "Crabrawler, use Bubble Beam!"

Ash asked Rowlet to dodge, and then use Peck. Rowlet's first moves proved successful, but Kahuna Hala soon picked up on Ash and Rowlet's tactics and countered them well. Crabrawler used its strong, sharp claws to grab Rowlet mid-attack. Then, with Brutal Swing, Crabrawler could swing Rowlet around and around and fling the other Pokémon high in the sky, nearly stunning it.

As the fight went on, Crabrawler's attack power only increased.

"That one's strong," Ash mumbled after Rowlet's Leafage move didn't do any damage to Crabrawler at all.

"I think you know by now that my Pokémon are trained far beyond what you're used to, my young Ash," Kahuna Hala declared.

Watching, Professor Kukui had to agree. Kahuna Hala's Pokémon were trained to the top of their abilities.

Ash felt bewildered. What could he do? What move might catch Hala and his mighty Crabrawler off guard?

Just then, Rowlet fluttered down near Ash's shoulder, surprising him. "Ah! Stop!" Ash cried. "You're always showing up that way, and I have no clue . . ."

Ash suddenly stopped and smiled at Rowlet. His stealthy Pokémon had helped him come up with a plan!

"Okay, Rowlet," Ash told his teammate quietly. "You're going to use Leafage one more time, but you'll scare Crabrawler when you do it!"

Rowlet seemed to understand at once. It released Leafage as soon as it started to dive toward Crabrawler. The glowing green leaves swirled around in a forceful wind, aimed right at Crabrawler.

Hala watched, confused about why Ash would try the same move again. He called for the attack that had been so successful against

Leafage last time. "Crabrawler, Bubble Beam!" he called.

Crabrawler's move hit Leafage head-on, creating a giant, hazy cloud. But when the cloud cleared away, Crabrawler could not find Rowlet.

Rowlet had sneaked up right behind him, and Ash ordered Peck, Peck, and more Peck!

Rowlet's attacks were working. Crabrawler was too exhausted to dodge.

"Now that's effective!" Rotom Dex cheered.

Hala ordered a Power-Up Punch. "Crabrawler, grab Rowlet and use Brutal Swing!"

"Be careful, Rowlet!" Ash advised. "Tackle, let's go!"

At the exact moment that Crabrawler lifted its claw, letting down its guard, Rowlet aimed a Tackle that sent the Fighting-type Pokémon flying. Crabrawler landed with a thud.

Professor Kukui rushed over to check on Crabrawler's condition. "Crabrawler is unable to battle!" he called out.

But the battle was still far from over.

CHAPTER 10

Kahuna Hala returned Crabrawler to its Poké Ball. "You battled valiantly," he told his teammate. Then he readied himself for the remainder of the grand trial.

Back on Ash's side of the arena, they were having a small celebration when Rotom Dex realized that Rowlet had fallen asleep. Ash tried to wake his teammate, but it was no use. It was exhausted from its strong showing in the battle with Crabrawler.

Ash sighed and got out Rowlet's Poké Ball. "Rowlet, you really did an awesome job, but we can take it from here."

After Rowlet was safely returned, Ash looked to Pikachu. Kahuna Hala had already tapped Hariyama as his next Pokémon.

Rotom Dex shared the data. "Hariyama, the Arm Thrust Pokémon, a Fighting-type. Hariyama's impressive bulk is actually all muscle. When its muscles are flexed, they are hard as a rock. It is said that one hit from a Hariyama can send a ten-ton truck flying."

"I'm counting on you, buddy," Ash told Pikachu as his partner jumped up on his shoulder. "I choose you!"

Pikachu pounced to the ground as Hariyama grunted a challenge.

Hariyama easily deflected Pikachu's first move of Iron Tail with Fake Out, followed quickly by Knock Off. Rotom and Professor Kukui agreed that it was a smart move combination.

Pikachu was determined, but even Electro Ball didn't do a thing. Hariyama countered with Arm Thrust and then kept throwing thrusts, batting Pikachu back and forth.

Pikachu took a huge amount of damage. Even when it slipped by Hariyama and landed a direct hit with Thunderbolt, the move had no effect.

Ash knew his only remaining move was the Z-Move, but he also knew he needed to choose the right time to use it.

On the other end of the arena, Kahuna Hala had decided it was his and Hariyama's time.

Hala called for Belly Drum, a move that maximizes a Pokémon's strength but uses up a lot of stamina. Then he belted out, "Here we go . . . do it!"

At once, Hala and Hariyama began to make the same graceful but powerful moves, sliding their legs in the air, stomping their feet, and flexing their arms.

"Is that . . . a Z-Move?" Ash asked out loud.

"Correct," declared Hala. "I make the wills of myself, Melemele, and Tapu Koko as one." He paused and took a deep breath. Then he and Hariyama began throwing fiery punches. "I . . . am . . . the . . . ka–hu–na! This is the moment when our strengths become one!"

"Pikachu, use Quick Attack!" Ash directed. "Dodge that Z-Move."

"*Pika!*" Pikachu ran straight at Hariyama.

"All-Out Pummeling!" Hala commanded. "Let's go!"

Pikachu ran head-on, dodging the constant attacks from Hariyama. But its final blast landed, sending Pikachu tumbling.

Luckily, Pikachu recovered quickly. Ash knew he needed to deal some damage, so he devised

a combination attack, "Pikachu! Quick Attack!
One more time!"

This time, Pikachu circled around and
around Hariyama, confusing the much larger
Pokémon. "Now use Iron Tail!"

When Pikachu zapped Hariyama's ankle, the
Arm Thrust Pokémon dropped to its knees.

"Hariyama took damage from that!" Rotom
Dex announced.

"Well, I guess it took a combination to fight a combination," Professor Kukui noted.

"Great job, Pikachu!" Ash cheered. At that moment, he knew the time had come. "Now it's our turn!"

Ash and Pikachu both crossed their arms, and electric pulses began to crackle around them. Ash's Z-Ring glowed with power. The two began their sequence of moves that drew from the mystical energy of the ring.

"It's happening. Pikachu and I are becoming one and that's making us much stronger than

either one of us!" Ash cried. "Here we go! Full power, now!"

Pikachu took off like a bolt, leaving smoke in its trail. "Breakneck Blitz!" Ash cried. Hariyama had no time to get out of the way.

"*Pika pi pi pi pi pi pi pi pi!*" Pikachu came at it like a comet, a bright center with a tail of flame. It was a direct hit!

"That was awesome, Pikachu! We used a Z-Move!" Ash could hardly believe it!

Professor Kukui assessed the damage to their opponent. "Melemele Kahuna Hala's Hariyama is unable to battle!" he said. "Which means the winner of this Melemele grand trial is the challenger, Ash Ketchum!"

"Ash wins the trial. Hooray!" Rotom celebrated.

Kahuna Hala thanked Hariyama as he returned the Pokémon to its Poké Ball. Then he turned to Ash. "I thoroughly enjoyed our splendid battle, young Ash. You and Rowlet and Pikachu gave it everything you had."

"Thank you very much, sir," Ash replied.

"*Pika pika chu!*" cheered Pikachu.

"As far as your Z-Move?" Hala continued. "It overflowed with the joy of accomplishment. I marveled at feeling your youthful, yet experienced, aura."

Ash smiled. The kahuna liked to speak in flowery language, but Ash could tell it was a supreme compliment.

"So, as the Melemele Island Kahuna, I hereby proclaim that Ash Ketchum has passed the grand trial!"

"All right!" Ash exclaimed with a clenched fist.

"Good for you," the kahuna said. "But please don't forget to take this." Then he held out his hand, and Ash caught a glimpse of a Z-Crystal. "It's your Fightinium Z. With this Z-Crystal, you'll be able to use the Fighting-type Z-Move."

"Awesome! Thank you!" Ash replied.

But before he could take the Z-Crystal, a high call trilled over the trees and there was a rush of wind that whooshed all around.

"What was that?" Ash wondered.

"Could that have been . . . Tapu Koko?" Professor Kukui said.

"It was so fast, I have no data," Rotom Dex stated.

When Kahuna Hala looked back at the crystal in his hand, it had changed! "It can't be!" he said.

"An Electrium Z?" Ash said, looking at the gem. "That looks just like the one I got from Tapu Koko!"

"Fascinating!" Hala exclaimed. "In all of my experience, this is the first time Tapu Koko has taken so much interest in a challenger. Eventually, I'll learn why. For now, I believe that this Electrium Z belongs to you. Take this Z-Crystal and use it with wisdom!"

"I will," Ash promised. "This Z-Crystal is all mine! An Electrium Z!"

That night, Kahuna Hala hosted a grand celebration for Ash and his friends from the Pokémon School. After all, without their help, Ash might not have learned the secret to

banishing the Rattata and Raticate. That had been just one stage of his Island Challenge. Each accomplishment had been part of the adventure. And with each step, Ash was discovering more about all he would learn on his journey to becoming a Pokémon Master!

Flip over this book for another awesome Pokémon story!

**Flip over this book for another
awesome Pokémon story!**